PUFFIN

Green Willow's Secret

Eileen Dunlop was born in Alloa in 1938 and educated at Alloa Academy and Moray House College. She is now a full-time writer and her books have been published all around the world including the USA, Irish Republic, Austria, Denmark, Sweden, Japan and South Africa. Her husband is also a writer.

# Green Willow's Secret

## Eileen Dunlop

PUFFIN BOOKS

PUFFIN BOOKS

Published by the Penguin Group
Penguin Books Ltd, 27 Wrights Lane, London W8 5TZ, England
Penguin Books USA Inc., 375 Hudson Street, New York, New York 10014, USA
Penguin Books Australia Ltd, Ringwood, Victoria, Australia
Penguin Books Canada Ltd, 10 Alcorn Avenue, Toronto, Ontario, Canada M4V 3B2
Penguin Books (NZ) Ltd, 182–190 Wairau Road, Auckland 10, New Zealand

Penguin Books Ltd, Registered Offices: Harmondsworth, Middlesex, England

First published by Blackie Children's Books 1993
Published in Puffin Books 1995
1 3 5 7 9 10 8 6 4 2

Printed in England by Clays Ltd, St Ives plc

*For Antony, who gave me
an idea for Christmas*

# Contents

# ACKNOWLEDGEMENTS

I should like to thank my Japanese friend, Chihiro Nakagawa, for supplying the Japanese originals of the poems I have used in this book, for translating into Japanese the ema which is a clue to the mystery in the story, and for much helpful advice on matters Japanese.

I am grateful to Chihiro's father, Yoshio Nakagawa, for transcribing the poems and the ema.

My thanks are also due to Janet Carolan and Jonathan Quick, who told me about another Japanese garden.

The English versions of the poems come from *The Penguin Book of Japanese Verse*, translated by Geoffrey Bownas and Anthony Thwaite.

# 1

# The Japanese Garden

Kit stood hesitantly in her red quilted jacket, pushing her gloved hands deep into the pockets for extra warmth. She stared at the little brown path which forked from the muddy farm road, then disappeared suddenly into the mouth of a dark, thin tunnel through the trees. In the golden October when she had first come to Maddimoss, she had thought the path uninviting, and had avoided it. Now, in February, as the sun set behind the wood, and night shadows lengthened, it seemed positively sinister. Only intense curiosity had brought her this far, and now she wondered if she had enough courage to go on.

In school that morning, Miss Whitaker had been talking about Japan. She had been to an exhibition of Japanese art in Edinburgh, and had brought the catalogue to show to her class. One of the pictures showed a garden heavy with pink and white blossom, and people in colourful kimonos strolling appreciatively over the grass. Kit was looking at it when one of the other children said, 'Miss Whitaker, there's a Japanese garden at Maddimoss, where Kit lives.'

'No, there isn't,' said Kit, lifting her dark head.

Other voices joined in.

'Yes, there is. I've heard my mum talking about it.'

'It's ancient. About a hundred years old.'

'Nobody goes there now. It's haunted.'

'Who by?'

'A ghost, stupid.'

'There isn't a Japanese garden,' said Kit, irritated.

She had only lived at Maddimoss for a few months, but she knew what the garden was like. Lumpy lawns with crumbly molehills and unpruned roses, and nothing remotely like the picture in Miss Whitaker's catalogue. So she was taken aback when Miss Whitaker said, 'Actually they're right, Kit. I went to see it once with my father, when I was a little girl. There's a path through the wood on the left, between Maddimoss House and Whitewells Farm . . .'

Attention had turned to maths after that, but Kit, entranced by the picture of cherry blossom, had thought all day about the garden. The idea of there being such a place at Maddimoss was so exciting that she couldn't wait to get home and find it. But she had forgotten, until she saw it again, how unpleasant the path was, and now she was tempted to forget it, to run home and sit by the stove in the familiar kitchen, to wait, and perhaps come another day. After all, a little voice in her head reminded her, it wasn't important. More than a year had passed since Kit had found anything that happened important at all. Which was why it was strange that now, in spite of the voice, she took a deep breath and plunged bravely in among the trees. Later, she would wonder whether some unseen hand of fate had pushed her on. At the time, it was just something she felt she had to do.

The tunnel, enclosed by walls and a roof of tangled, unkempt conifers, was every bit as nasty as it had looked from the road. It was dark, damp and full of traps. Barbed branches whipped back in Kit's face as soon as she had pushed them aside. The soft, moist forest floor was laced with sharp-toothed brambles, which caught at her ankles and scored her bare legs, while the heady scent of pine and water made her feel dizzy and confused. More than once some mysterious rustling among the trees made her choke with terror, and the wild wing-whirr of a startled pheasant almost stopped her heart. All the time she wanted to go back, but somehow controlled herself, and struggled on. It could only have been ten minutes, yet it seemed hours before a shaft of bronze light pierced the gloom, and Kit stepped thankfully towards the sunset on the far side of the wood. Then she had her reward. The Japanese garden lay before her, not at all like the picture in Miss Whitaker's catalogue, but strange and wonderful beyond dreams.

In the middle of a clearing, sheared from the darkness of the surrounding wood, there was a small lake, its burnished surface spotted with floating lily pads. Around the lake, and in it – for it had two islands, and a fan of circular stepping-stones – was the garden, with pine trees and rhododendrons, and unleaved willows trailing their frail fingers along the water's edge. Slender bridges arched between the islands and the shore, where, to Kit's amazement, there were buildings. Frowning into the sun which blazed crimson through a gap in the trees, she saw huts with latticed panels, curving roofs and delicately upturned eaves. She was reminded of an old willow pattern plate her mother used to have in the kitchen, only that was blue and cool, and a picture. The scene before her, flushed deep pink and gold, was more extravagant by far. It was also real. Snatches of the conversation in school came back to Kit.

'Made by an old couple who used to live at Maddimoss House, my mum says. They went on holiday to Japan . . .'

'Nobody goes there now. It's haunted.'

Kit didn't believe in ghosts, but as she wandered round the lake, she could certainly believe that nobody came here now. Seen in close-up, the garden was sadly neglected. The trees and shrubs hadn't been pruned for years, the water in the lake was slimy, the bridges broken and unsafe. Miniature waterfalls, designed to cascade among gracefully arranged rocks, were stopped by an accumulation of moss and decayed leaves. Only thin trickles, like melting icicles, dripped miserably into stagnant pools.

Most distressing of all, the little huts – Kit saw two by the water, and glimpsed the roof of a third among the trees – were quietly falling apart. Much of the lattice was broken. There were rotting planks in the verandahs, and wooden tiles were missing from the roofs. Red and gold paint, used to pick out carved patterns under the eaves, was almost worn away. As she picked her way back through tattered flags of iris towards the wood, for a moment Kit was overwhelmed by the sadness of a place once beautiful, loved and cared for, but now, seemingly, forgotten.

Still, she was glad she had come, and she was determined she would come again – perhaps tomorrow, Saturday, when she was at a loose end. Kit was the only child at Maddimoss, and although she got on well enough with the other children at Tillyrie School, she hadn't made a special friend, the kind with whom you spend Saturday. She also decided, as she battled back along the tree-tunnel, that she would find out more about this exotic, forgotten place. It felt so mysterious, and thinking about it might help her to forget her troubles – if such a thing were possible now.

# 2

# Juliet

Kit went to bed that night thinking about the Japanese garden, but she dreamed of something else. She dreamed often, and the dream was always the same.

She and Juliet had gone swimming at the Commonwealth Pool, near where they had lived in Edinburgh. The pool was crowded and noisy, as it always was on Saturday. Kit was standing on the side, watching Juliet, who was in the deep water. Unnoticed by the merry, splashing crowd around her, Juliet was drowning. Kit watched her sink, then come to the surface, her thin arms thrashing, her face a pale green mask with silently screaming mouth and wide, terrified eyes. Twice she sank and came up again, then she went down for the last time. Kit saw her go, arms and legs paddling involuntarily, until she rested face down on the bottom of the pool. Her fair hair, drifting gently, was the only part of her which still looked alive. Then Kit, who had watched unmoving, turned and walked away.

As always, she had got as far as the changing-room when she woke suddenly, starting up in the darkness with a stifled cry. Her body was as wet as if she really had been swimming, oozing sweat which drenched her pyjamas and soaked coldly into her hair. Shakily she groped for the switch on her bedside lamp, turned on the light, and peered at her little alarm clock. It was ten past two.

Kit took off her pyjamas, dropped them on the floor and switched off the lamp. Curling up naked under her duvet, she wished with all her heart that she could say, 'Silly! It was only a dream,' yawn, and fall asleep again. But she couldn't. For Juliet was dead, as surely as if she had drowned in the swimming pool. Kit hadn't watched her; she had been nowhere near at the time of the accident. Yet she felt as guilty as if she had pushed Juliet in front of the van that had killed her. It had never occurred to her to wish her sister actual harm, but she had hated Juliet. She was not sorry that she was dead.

After the dream, there was the waking nightmare. Chilled and stiff, Kit lay in the darkness, fighting the memory of Juliet who had been dead for more than a year, but still dominated her family as powerfully as when she was alive. Juliet, fair and beautiful, her fragility contradicting the steely strength inside her. Juliet, the real daughter of her parents, who had given her Kit as a Christmas present when she was two. Of course Peter and Laura – they had never wanted to be called 'Dad' and 'Mum' – would have denied this indignantly, but they could hardly have blamed Kit for believing it. They had never tried to hide from her that she was adopted, and she had seen the announcement, cut from the newspaper and stuck into the pink photograph album which recorded her babyhood. *CRAWFORD: Peter and Laura are proud to announce the arrival of their daughter Catherine, born on 5 October, adopted on 23 December. A Christmas gift for Juliet*. They might deny that they had meant it, but they couldn't deny that they had said it. It had been there in black and white for all of Edinburgh to read.

Kit had always had a mental picture of herself as a baby, wrapped in gaudy paper instead of a shawl, left overnight under the Christmas tree for Juliet to find in the morning. She knew she wouldn't have been a favourite present. As they grew up together, Juliet had shown no sign of hating Kit. More offensively, except when Kit had something she wanted, she had scarcely seemed to notice that her sister was there.

Upstairs in old Miss Sorley's flat, the grandfather clock struck three. Laura said that its relentless chiming would drive her crazy, but this was Miss Sorley's house, which made it difficult to complain. Kit thought the clock was the least of their troubles. Her feet were like ice and she wanted to sleep, but the past was too vivid. She went on torturing herself.

To be fair, Peter and Laura had never been guilty of open favouritism. Kit's bedroom was as pretty as Juliet's, and Laura took as much trouble making a party frock to suit her small, dark, brown-eyed daughter as she did making one to suit her tall, fair, blue-eyed one. Peter took them both to the cinema, and it was made clear, when Juliet went to St George's School, that Kit would also go, when she was twelve. But when it came to getting real attention, Juliet won hands down. She had a weapon which Kit lacked. She coughed. If Kit had a toy she wanted, she coughed. If Kit beat her twice at Snakes and Ladders, she coughed. If she didn't want to go to PE, she coughed. And because she had asthma, and her parents were terrified to risk her having a bad attack, these little blackmailing coughs worked, every time.

'Come on, Kit. Be sporting,' Peter would say ridiculously. 'Let Juliet win next time.'

And, 'Well, never mind. If you aren't feeling up to it, I'll write a note to Mrs Frazer,' Laura would sigh, most Wednesday mornings.

They watched over Juliet with tender, fretful care.

'Darling, have you got your inhaler?'

'Juliet, have you got your boots on? Remember to take your scarf.'

Kit knew they weren't making a fuss about nothing. Juliet was really ill. Night after night, especially in winter, Kit had woken to see the landing light shining down the side of her bedroom door, and heard the terrible wheezing and gasping as her sister fought for breath in the room next door. She could hear Peter and Laura, gentle, trying to be reassuring. And she could picture Juliet, propped up in Laura's arms, while Peter sat on the side of the bed, pressing her hand and trying to comfort her. It was easy to imagine, because she had seen them, once. Aged seven and jealous, Kit had got out of bed and stumbled through to Juliet's room, where she stood blinking in the light.

'I need a drink of water,' she had said plaintively.

She would never forget what had happened next. Three pairs of eyes had turned on her, Juliet's indignant, Peter's reproachful, Laura's blazing with anger.

17

'For God's sake,' Laura had said harshly, 'get it yourself. Can't you see Juliet needs us?'

Next morning she had said she was sorry, explained how ill Juliet had been, and given Kit a cuddle. But Kit had not forgiven her, and she had never been able to feel sorry for Juliet after that. Passing Juliet's door, on her way downstairs in the morning, she would look in, and see Juliet sitting up on her pillows, her elfin face pinched and exhausted. She never spoke to Kit, but looked at her, Kit thought, with a little gleam of triumph in her cold blue eyes. It might have been triumph because she had come safely through another painful night, but Kit didn't think so. To her, it was the triumph of someone who knew that, whatever happened, she would always come first.

Miss Sorley's clock struck the half-hour. Kit heard Laura's bedroom door open softly, and saw a thin ribbon of light under her own. She heard Laura go into the kitchen, then, distantly, the sound of the poker stirring up the embers in the stove. Since Juliet's death, Laura had slept badly, and Kit often heard her moving about in the night. She supposed that Laura made tea, and sat by the stove, reading the paperback thrillers which were the only books she ever bought nowadays. Kit would have liked a cup of tea, but she had no intention of getting up and walking in on Laura, ever again. She turned over, and went on reliving the past.

Juliet had been in bed a lot during the winter. When Kit came home from school, she would find the downstairs rooms in darkness, and the fire out, because Laura was upstairs amusing Juliet. When

Peter came home he would put down his briefcase in the hall, rumple Kit's hair casually, then run upstairs two at a time to Juliet's room. Kit remembered the doting tone of his voice.

'Hello, my love. How has my girl been today?'

Then, one dark December afternoon, when there were Christmas trees in the windows of Mayfield Road, and Juliet had been well enough to go to school every day since half-term, life changed suddenly, and for ever.

Juliet had come home from school on the bus. Getting off in Minto Street, and waving to a friend who was travelling on, she had stepped carelessly from the pavement into the path of a delivery van. Witnesses to the accident had said the driver didn't have a chance. They had seen his horrified face as he stood on the brakes, swerved, skidded and hit Juliet, before crashing into a lamp-post. Juliet's crumpled body was lifted into an ambulance, and rushed, with siren screaming, to the Royal Infirmary.

Kit, arriving home late after a rehearsal of the school Nativity play, had found their neighbour, Mrs Arthur, in the kitchen. She had known at once that something was wrong.

'Where's Laura?' she had demanded suspiciously.

'Oh, my dear.' Mrs Arthur had looked really distressed. 'Such bad news. I'm afraid she's had to go to the Infirmary. Poor little Juliet has had an accident.'

Tossing about in the dark at Maddimoss, fourteen months later, Kit remembered the kindly, anxious face, the arms waiting to go round her when she cried out in sisterly grief. She also remembered what had actually happened.

Hurling her school bag violently across the floor, she had rushed out of the kitchen, up the stairs and into her room, where she threw herself on the bed, sobbing with anger and frustration. It was so unfair. In ten days it would be Christmas, and there would be Juliet, on crutches with a broken leg, the centre of attention once again. There would be flowers, and get-well cards, and extra presents, and golden-haired Juliet smirking on the sofa like a pussy that had swallowed a lot of cream. While rosy, sturdy Kit moped in the background, ignored and in the way. Her hatred of Juliet reached its peak that winter afternoon, when Juliet was already lying dead in the Royal Infirmary.

Mrs Arthur came upstairs three times, but Kit refused to speak to her, so she went away again. Kit was still lying face down on the bed when Peter came, groping across the dark room to take her in his arms and sob out the news that she didn't have a sister any more. Because his grief frightened her, Kit wept with him, and went on joining in with all the weeping adults through the terrible days that followed. At Juliet's funeral she cried out loud, and everyone said how close the two sisters must have been.

Outside the wind rose, and rain spattered fitfully on the window. Kit heard Miss Sorley's clock strike five, and Laura go back to bed, before she fell asleep. She woke again at eight, and found the sheet still damp with guilt and fear.

# 3

# An Old
# Photograph

The stove had gone out, and the vast, stone-floored kitchen was icily cold, so when Kit had made her breakfast she took it into the sitting-room. There was no sign of Laura, who usually slept late these days. Outside, the wind was soughing in the bare branches of the trees, and rain ran down the window-panes like tears. Sometimes Kit went for long, solitary walks at the weekends, but today a walk was out of the question, as – she felt a sharp little stab of regret – was another visit to the Japanese garden. But also out of the question was a long, tedious day spent alone, cooped up in this house where nothing belonged to her. So Kit decided that after breakfast she would go to visit her friend Mrs Maxwell at Whitewells Farm. She had remembered that Mr and Mrs Maxwell had lived all their lives at Maddimoss, so they would certainly have information about the Japanese garden. Fortunately she could get to Whitewells in less than five minutes, if she ran.

The sitting-room wasn't much warmer than the kitchen. Kit drank her coffee and munched her toast huddled on the rug in front of a feeble electric fire, which burnt her back and left the rest of her freezing.

The wind, howling in the unused chimney, blew ill-tempered gusts from the cavernous grate, so that even the velvet curtains shook in the draught. What a dump, Kit thought gloomily. She hated Maddi-moss House, with its carved ebony tables, huge chests of drawers and walls dark with heavily patterned paper. Every flat surface was covered with orna-ments, so that you could hardly see the spaces in between. Brought up in a house with white walls, sparse furniture and wide wooden floors, Kit some-times felt she would suffocate.

Of course, she hadn't blamed Laura for refusing to spend another Christmas in Edinburgh, reliving the hell of the last one. She hadn't wanted to either, and it was bad luck that the new house Peter was building had been plagued with delays. All the same, they had come to this ghastly rented flat in October, believing that their new house would be ready in January. Instead it was still a forlorn, roofless shell, standing in a nearby field which Peter had bought from Miss Sorley, while the builder muttered feebly about a problem with the drains. And because Peter had gone to Australia for three months, and Laura was afraid of the builder, nothing at all was being done.

It was too cold to linger, so Kit finished her break-fast quickly. She thought she would make her bed, and stoke up the stove, so that the kitchen would be warm when she got back from Whitewells. But as she was opening the door, her attention was caught by something she must have seen dozens of times, but had never really noticed. Letting the door swing shut again, she stood holding her mug and plate, and staring with intense interest.

Hanging on the dark green wall by the door was an old-fashioned photograph of the Japanese garden. It was at once recognizable as the place where Kit had walked yesterday, in the flush of the dying sun. She saw the steep, winged roofs, the bridges and the white stepping-stones, graceful as a flight of birds across the water. But this was the garden in its young days. The trees were smaller, and the shrubs clipped into sharp shapes. Kit could make out paths and groups of stones which had now vanished into the undergrowth. Everything was lovingly tended, and clearly defined.

What fascinated Kit most, however, was that there were people in the picture. In the foreground, standing stiffly, were an elderly couple in straw hats, with a black spaniel at their feet. The lady was wearing a longish dress of some droopy material, the gentleman a dark suit with a waistcoat, and a gold watch chain. Further back, on a bridge, there was a third figure. He was a slender, good-looking young man, dressed in a short, wide-sleeved robe, belted over loose trousers. His feet were in sandals, held on by thongs between his toes. Under a thick sweep of hair, long dark eyes smiled shyly into the camera. Kit knew it was silly to be surprised by the sight of a Japanese in a Japanese garden. But this garden was at Maddimoss, half-way between Perth and Dundee.

Underneath the photograph a little printed card was stuck to the dull gold mount. It said: *Mr and Mrs John Sorley in their Japanese garden, August 1932.* Kit took her mug and plate into the kitchen, and thoughtfully rinsed them under the tap.

She was making her bed when something else

23

occurred to her. It was another thing about this house that she had seen without being in the least interested, or wanting to look twice. It was full of things from Japan. Most of the ornaments on the bookcases and chests of drawers were from the east, porcelain vases, jade and ivory miniatures, black lacquer boxes and dozens of fans. Kit had once heard Laura remark that they would be wonderful if there were only a few of them, instead of enough to stock ten museums. Again Kit remembered the comment at school, about the old couple who went on holiday to Japan. Of course, they must have been Mr and Mrs John Sorley. They had made a Japanese garden outside, and had filled their house with holiday souvenirs. Making this connection excited Kit; she was pleased by the feeling that she was beginning to find things out. When she had put logs into the stove, she put on her coat and boots, and scampered off up the muddy, rutted track to Whitewells Farm. She had to hold down her hood against the wind and driving rain.

## 4

## The Foundling
## of Maddimoss

Kit loved the kitchen at Whitewells, with its shelves
laden with pitchers and blue crockery, and cats sleeping sleekly on the red rug in front of the fire. There
was always a delicious smell of soup or stew cooking
on the stove; in Kit's house there was only ever the
fugitive, ten-minute odour of Marks and Spencer's
oven-ready meals. Mrs Maxwell, a large, comfortable
woman whose own children were grown up and
away at college, was always glad to see Kit, and the
farmer himself, though he spoke little, welcomed her
amiably.

'Now come away in, dear,' said Mrs Maxwell,
when Kit appeared at the yard door, 'and take off
that wet coat. What a terrible day! Dad's just in
from the milking, and I'm making him a cup of tea.
Will you have tea like him, or coffee like me?'

'Coffee, please,' said Kit, exchanging grins with
Mr Maxwell, who was sitting by the fire in his shirt-
sleeves, and smelling strongly of cow.

Kit sat opposite Mrs Maxwell at the long table,
drinking her coffee and helping herself from a plate
of freshly baked cookies, which was placed hospitably
in front of her. She waited for Mrs Maxwell's usual,
'And what have you been doing since I saw you

last?' then answered quickly, 'I've been to the Japanese garden.'

She saw surprise in her friend's grey eyes.

'The Japanese garden,' repeated Mrs Maxwell softly. 'That old place. I'd almost forgotten it existed. How on earth did you find it, Kit?'

Kit explained how, following Miss Whitaker's directions, she had battled along the dark path through the wood.

'It's hardly a path at all now,' she said. 'I don't think anyone's used it for years.'

'No,' agreed Mrs Maxwell, 'I don't suppose anyone has.' She smiled at Kit and added teasingly, 'You were very brave, Kit. The garden's supposed to be haunted.'

It was the second time Kit had heard this.

'I don't believe in ghosts,' she said firmly. But then, as the memory of her fear in the wood, and the garden's melancholy, returned to her, she added, 'It's a strange place, though. Beautiful, but sad and lonely too. Who does it belong to, Mrs Maxwell?'

Mrs Maxwell laughed dryly.

'It belongs to Miss Sorley,' she said. 'She's sold off everything else around here these last few years, including Whitewells to Dad and me. But the Japanese garden's just a marsh. No one would want to buy that.'

There was a hard little edge in Mrs Maxwell's usually pleasant voice which told Kit she didn't much care for Miss Sorley.

'There's a picture of the Japanese garden in our sitting-room,' Kit said. 'It was taken in 1932, and there are Sorleys in it, Mr and Mrs John Sorley. Did they make the garden?'

Mrs Maxwell nodded.

'That's so,' she confirmed. 'Went travelling in the east and got wild ideas. More money than sense, if you ask me.'

This opinion didn't surprise Kit in the least. She knew that Mrs Maxwell, a shrewd farmer's wife, would never waste time growing anything she couldn't sell at the market in Dundee. Kit disagreed, but she didn't want to have an argument. So she turned the subject slightly by saying, 'And they would be Miss Sorley's parents, of course.'

This seemed obvious to her.

But, 'No,' said Mrs Maxwell emphatically. 'They were not. For all the airs and graces that lady gives herself, she's not really a Sorley at all.'

Kit was puzzled.

'Not really a Sorley?' she repeated, wrinkling her brows. 'What is she, then?'

Mrs Maxwell put her plump elbows on the table, and leaned forward confidentially.

'Nobody knows,' she said impressively. 'She was a foundling. That's what a baby's called if it's found and brought up by strangers,' she added, in case Kit didn't know.

Kit did know, and felt as if she were listening to a fairy tale.

'Who found her?' she asked, fixing astonished brown eyes on Mrs Maxwell's face.

'It was the Sorleys' cook,' replied Mrs Maxwell, enjoying the success of her story-telling. 'Can you imagine it, Kit? Miss Sorley was found on the back doorstep at Maddimoss House when she was a tiny baby. My mother was a young maid to Mrs Sorley, just fifteen, and often she told me how the cook heard a baby crying, and when she opened the door, there the creature was, wrapped in a shawl on the doormat. The Sorleys were past their youth, but they took the baby in, and brought her up, and gave her their own name. She was sent to a grand boarding school, and when the old couple died they left her everything – Maddimoss House, and this farm, and Sparrowlea, and Frankly Woods, and Inch of Tilly, and the Japanese garden. Oh, and a big house in London, so I've heard tell. Nobody knows who she is, or where she came from, but she did pretty well out of the Sorleys, wouldn't you say?'

Kit couldn't say. She was speechless with amazement. Of course, she had sometimes heard on the news of babies found outside hospitals, or in telephone kiosks, so it did happen. But old Miss Sorley? Perhaps the most difficult thing was to believe that she had ever been a baby at all.

'All of which being so,' concluded Mrs Maxwell sniffily, 'it's hard to understand why the lady's so high and mighty that she can't pass the time of day with her neighbours.'

Kit realized that this was a sore point. But before she could say anything Mr Maxwell, who had been drinking his tea and reading *Farming Weekly*, unexpectedly came to Miss Sorley's defence.

'Ach, Maggie,' he said, poking out his head from behind the paper, 'you're too hard on Miss Sorley. She was a fair landlord, and she sold us the farm at a very reasonable price. And if she's shy, and won't take tea with her neighbours, who's to blame her? Would you not be sick and tired of folk gossiping behind your back, and envying you for what you couldn't help? Do you know Miss Sorley, Kit?' he asked, ignoring the deepening colour in his wife's cheeks, and the annoyed pursing of her mouth.

Kit shook her head.

'Not really. She came down the first night we were here,' she said. She had a sudden, vivid memory of Miss Sorley that evening, a tiny old woman with slate-grey hair twisted into a knot on the crown of her head, and shy eyes protected by darkly tinted spectacles. Invited by Peter to sit down, she had hovered tentatively, like a little bird in her brown dress, on the edge of a chair. It had been obvious that she didn't intend to settle. After apologizing for the quirkiness of the central heating, and telling Laura the arrangements for buying milk, she had departed, and apart from a cool, 'Good morning', none of the Crawfords had heard a word from her since. 'She didn't speak to me,' Kit told Mr Maxwell, wondering why on earth that thought should make her sad.

'She doesn't speak to anyone,' said Mrs Maxwell sourly, sweeping up the coffee cups and taking them to the sink.

Trying not to laugh at Mr Maxwell's comical winking, Kit followed her and picked up a dishtowel. Mr Maxwell folded his paper, pulled on his waterproof, and crossed to the door. As he went out into the rain Mrs Maxwell turned, glared at his departing back, and stuck out her tongue like a little girl. Then she laughed heartily, and Kit joined in.

'I have to go to the butcher's in Tillyrie,' said Mrs Maxwell, drying her hands on her apron. 'Do you want to come along for the ride?'

Kit shook her head.

'I'd like to, but no, thanks,' she said. 'My mum doesn't know where I am. I'd better get back.'

She was buttoning up her coat when it occurred to her that she'd learned a lot more about Miss Sorley that morning than she had about the Japanese garden. There was only time now for one more question.

'Mrs Maxwell,' she said. 'In the photograph at our house, the one with Mr and Mrs Sorley in the garden, there's a young Japanese man standing on a bridge. Do you know who he was?'

Mrs Maxwell looked surprised.

'Oh, is there?' she said. 'I thought I knew the photograph you meant. All the families on the estate got one on their silver wedding, I think it was. They always did act like royalty. But there wasn't a Japanese in it, just them and their dog. Yours must be a different one.'

'So?' prompted Kit.

'They had a gardener from Japan,' Mrs Maxwell told her. 'Dead before I was born, and I forget his name. He died young. His grave's in Frankly churchyard, down in the corner behind the Sorleys' tomb.'

# 5

# A Silk
# Shawl

Laura got up at lunchtime, and came into the kitchen in her dressing-gown. She sat down at the table, shivered, and ran long fingers through her unkempt fair hair. Kit watched her running tired eyes over the shabby green walls and empty shelves, and steeled herself for an outburst of moaning about the awfulness of Maddimoss House, and how Laura wished they were anywhere but here. Today, however, it didn't come.

'I'm sorry, love,' Laura said to Kit. 'I have a dreadful headache. Can you get yourself something to eat, and bring me a cup of tea?'

'Of course,' agreed Kit, to whom this had become the normal Saturday routine.

Since moving from Edinburgh to his company's Dundee office, Peter had had to go away often, on business. Now he was on the other side of the world, and added to the problems that gave Laura headaches was a new one, the possibility that he wouldn't come back. In the year following Juliet's death, Peter and Laura had quarrelled constantly, and when Peter had been asked to go to Sydney for three months, both had found it difficult to hide their relief. But Peter had scarcely written, and slowly it had dawned on Laura that she and Kit might have been abandoned in a gloomy rented flat, five miles from anywhere, and with no prospect of getting their new house completed. It was no wonder she had headaches, and Kit didn't really blame her for staying in bed, when she had so little worth getting up for.

'Do you want a slice of toast?' Kit asked.

'Good of you,' said Laura, giving her a brief smile, 'but no, thanks.'

Kit watched her getting up and shuffling towards the door, and had to harden her heart. It was difficult not to feel sorry for someone so unhappy. Sometimes she wished that Laura would lose her temper, and shout, and give Kit an up-to-date reason for not loving her. But although she had yelled at Peter, nowadays Laura was always gentle with Kit, and Kit knew why. Deceived by appearances at the time of Juliet's death, Laura believed that Kit had loved her sister, and was grieving too. Her kindness made Kit feel more guilty than ever.

But it wasn't going to make her change her mind, she told herself fiercely, as she switched on the electric kettle, and tossed a tea-bag into a mug. Her plan was made, and she would carry it out, whether Peter came back from Australia or not. In four and a half years' time, when she was sixteen, she was going to leave, and never come back. She was going to find her real mother, the teenager who, Laura said, had given up her baby so that she could be free to go to university. Only she wouldn't be a teenager now, and Kit had convinced herself easily that the unknown young woman longed for the baby she hadn't chosen to keep. Kit imagined constantly their meeting, the surprise, the warmth, the growing affection as they got to know each other. As she poured boiling water into Laura's mug, she suddenly saw in her mind's eye shy, solitary Miss Sorley, another adopted child. Never, Kit vowed, would she be like her. Kit Crawford, who wasn't really a Crawford, would find out who she was.

Thoughts of escape had kept hope alive in Kit through a terrible year, while Peter and Laura fought and drifted apart, and dreams of Juliet made her wake sweating in the dark. If Laura had wanted to be loved, she should have behaved differently. Now it was too late.

After she had taken Laura her tea, and made herself a bacon sandwich, Kit drifted into the sitting-room. The morning's rain had turned to sleet, which was blotching the window with weeping circles, and distorting the wind-raked garden outside. The afternoon stretched endlessly ahead, and Kit thought listlessly that she might as well switch on the electric fire and watch a video film. The Crawfords had brought their television and video-recorder with them to Maddimoss; all their other belongings were in store in Dundee.

Kit was sorting through the pile of cassettes, looking in vain for a film she hadn't watched at least four times before, when her eyes were drawn sideways to a small black lacquered box. It was a beautiful thing, heart-shaped and decorated with bird and blossom in muted gold and green. Next to it on the table was a little cabinet carved like a gilded temple, and because she didn't really want to watch a film, and one thing led to another, Kit found herself wandering round the room, picking up boxes, fingering vases, shaking open fans.

With her new-found interest in Japan, she reckoned that Laura was right. Looked at one at a time, these were magical things. She had been round the room twice when she found herself standing in front of an enormous chest of drawers. Rather to her surprise, she realized that she was dying to know what was in it. In the last year, Kit had rarely felt curious about anything; it was as if all her energy was consumed by misery. Finding the Japanese garden had suddenly made her inquisitive again.

The chest of drawers was ugly, and Kit thought it was too big to be Japanese. But it looked eastern, with a dull gold pattern of bamboo across its five black, brass-handled drawers. Kit knew that she could open them and rummage through the contents without anyone knowing, yet for a moment she held back. She knew that, just as you shouldn't open other people's desks at school, you probably shouldn't open drawers in someone else's house. But then she remembered something Miss Sorley had said, when poised for flight after her brief visit. Glancing round the sitting-room as if it bewildered her, she had remarked to Laura, 'One day soon I'll have to go through this place, and make a list of what's actually here. Only I keep putting off the evil hour. So please, if you're short of anything, feel free to look, and help yourself.' Deciding that these words were as good as an invitation, Kit dragged over a chair, stood on it and opened the top drawer.

The chest, however, proved a disappointment. It

didn't contain treasure. Kit found only tarnished cutlery, old gardening magazines, crumbling candles and discoloured table linen. Not until she had worked her way right down to the bottom did she find anything interesting, and it was nothing Japanese.

In the last drawer there was a battered brown cardboard box. When Kit took off the lid, she found baby clothes, carefully folded. First she shook out an embroidered robe, its cascading lace lemon with age. Underneath there was a frilly bonnet and a pair of tiny lace mittens. Finally there was a shawl, which Kit spread out on the floor. Although it was white, it wasn't a baby shawl of the usual woolly kind. It was made of silk, loosely woven into a pattern of flowers and finished with fringes like long, fine hair. In one corner, embroidered in red, were the letters Y A N A G I. Kit traced them with her finger, wondering what they meant. It was obvious from the different stitching that they were not part of the original design.

It was impossible, looking at these old and lovely garments, not to think of Miss Sorley, who had been found on the back doorstep – how long ago? Kit supposed the old lady was about seventy. Had the clothes belonged to her? Kit thought it was unlikely that a poor child would have been abandoned in such finery, so perhaps the Sorleys had bought the robe for her christening. But it was the letters, Y A N A G I, that intrigued her most. What on earth could they mean? And why did she have this extraordinary feeling that she had seen them somewhere before?

Kit folded the robe, and put it back in the box with the bonnet and mittens. She was going to lay the shawl on top, but then decided on impulse that she would borrow it for a while. It was beautiful, and would help to liven up her dull bedroom, if she pinned it carefully to the wall.

Kit closed the drawer, hung the shawl over her arm, and walked over to the door. As she opened it, she glanced at the picture of the Japanese garden – then stopped, and stared in bewilderment. Mr and Mrs John Sorley looked placidly out from the edge of the lake, just as they had done for more than sixty years. But the young Japanese whom Kit had seen that morning, standing behind them on the little bridge, had now disappeared.

# 6

# The
# Stranger

At eleven o'clock on Sunday morning, Kit left the
house to walk to Frankly churchyard. It wasn't the
day she would have chosen for an expedition;
although the rain was holding off, the sky scowled,
and the east wind was roaring up the Carse, the
plain between the river Tay and the upland Braes,
which held Maddimoss in a tuck at their foot. But
she just had to get out for a while, and go somewhere.
The way she was feeling, almost anywhere would
do.

Annoyed with herself, but unable to resist, Kit
had spent all her waking hours since yesterday afternoon padding to and fro between the kitchen and
the sitting-room, peeping round the door at the
photograph where at nine o'clock on Saturday morning there had been a young Japanese, and now there
was not. She wasn't sure whether she expected him
to return, but anyway, he didn't. The bridge
remained empty, and when she remembered Mrs
Maxwell's surprise at her mention of the Japanese,
Kit came close to believing that she had never seen
him at all.

But not quite. As she walked down the farm track
towards the main road, her eyes watering in the

bitter wind, the sheer vividness of the memory convinced Kit that she hadn't been mistaken. The young man had been so distinct in his wide-sleeved robe, with his long dark eyes and shyly friendly expression. How could she possibly have such a detailed picture in her mind, if she hadn't seen him with her own eyes? And if she had – Kit knew this was the big question – was she then admitting that she, who had never believed in ghosts, had now actually seen one? Could a photograph be haunted? Of course you couldn't ask anyone such a question. That would be to invite forehead tapping, and funny looks. But it was difficult not to believe what you were sure you had seen.

The mournful tolling of Frankly church bell was carried fitfully on the gusting wind, but long before she got to Frankly Kit realized that she wouldn't find the Japanese gardener's grave that day. The wind began to spit in her face, and down across the Carse she could see another sleet storm advancing, like a flittering grey curtain. She was half-way back when it caught up with her, and by the time she got home she was soaked and shivering. But still the first thing she did was to open the sitting-room door, and check on the missing person. Of course, he hadn't returned. Close to screaming, Kit went off to the bathroom to dry her hair. How she was to get through the rest of the day without a diversion, she didn't know. But, as it happened, a diversion was on the way.

Laura had summoned enough energy today to get up, and exchange her dressing-gown for a crumpled green tracksuit. Sometimes Kit wondered if she still possessed the embroidered velvet dresses and jewel-coloured tights she had worn in happier days. Laura had heated up a tin of tomato soup, and made some ham sandwiches. She and Kit watched a chat show on the old portable television on the dresser as they ate, because it was easier than making conversation. The storm had wrapped itself around the house like a grey blanket, and the windows were black against the electric light.

'I'll make coffee,' said Laura, but before she had time to lift the kettle and put it under the tap, someone knocked loudly on the back door.

Kit jumped.

'Who on earth can that be?' she said, getting up and switching off the television.

Laura shrugged, put down the kettle, and went to open the door. Against the whirling sleet, Kit saw a boy standing on the doorstep. He was tall and thin, in wet denim jeans and a dark waterproof jacket, its hood drawn tightly around his pale, grey-eyed face. The sleet was melting on his hood and trickling down his cheeks, and when he spoke he could scarcely keep his teeth from chattering.

'I'm sorry to bother you,' said the boy politely, 'but is your name Maddimoss?' Even in his discomfort he sounded eager, and when Laura shook her head Kit could see how disappointed he was. 'Oh, no,' he groaned. 'And I thought − when I saw the sign at the end of the road −'

'It's the name of the house,' Laura explained. Then, as a gust of sleety air wrapped itself around her ankles, she added hastily, 'You'd better come inside. It isn't weather for chatting on doorsteps.'

Gratefully the boy stepped into the kitchen.

'My name is Daniel. Daniel Garth,' he said, in a voice with a strong English accent.

'I'm Laura Crawford, and this is my daughter Kit,' replied Laura. 'Now take off your jacket, and come and sit by the stove.'

Daniel obeyed gladly. Under his jacket he was wearing a brown and black striped sweater; his hair was brown and curly, and he had a gold earring in his left ear. No, he said, he hadn't had lunch, and yes, he'd love a pizza and the rest of the tomato soup. While he dried his face on a towel and stood in front of the stove to dry his jeans, Laura laid a place at the end of the table, and Kit put a frozen pizza in the microwave. She felt quite excited by the arrival of this youthful stranger. Visitors to Maddimoss House were few and far between, and here was the diversion she had been longing for.

When the pizza and a mug of soup were placed in front of him, Daniel ate as if he hadn't seen food for a week. In less than five minutes he laid down his knife and fork, grinned for the first time, and said, 'That was great. Thanks. I'm sorry your name isn't Maddimoss, but you've been very kind.'

It went through Kit's mind that it had been quite a weekend for mysteries, one way and another.

Laura made three mugs of coffee, and brought them to the table. She opened the biscuit tin, and put it between Daniel and Kit.

'I've never heard of anyone being called Maddimoss,' she said thoughtfully, as she stirred her coffee. 'I don't think it's that kind of name, is it?'

'It was my granny's name,' Daniel told her. 'She

was a Miss Maddimoss before she married my grandad. I'm looking for –' He hesitated for a split second, and Kit knew that for some reason he had altered what he was going to say. 'I'm looking for a member of my granny's family. Someone she asked me to contact, before she died.'

'Was your granny Scottish?' asked Kit, addressing Daniel for the first time.

Daniel nodded.

'She went to London when she was very young,' he said, 'and worked as a maid in the house where my grandad was footman. I thought I'd find lots of Maddimosses in the telephone directory here, but I haven't found one. That was why I was so excited when I passed this morning, and saw a sign saying "Maddimoss".' He took a gulp of coffee, then asked, 'Who lived in this house before you, Mrs Crawford?'

Laura explained that it wasn't her house.

'We rent the downstairs from the old lady who lives upstairs,' she said. 'Her name is Sorley.'

'And the Sorleys have lived here for more than a hundred years,' put in Kit, who had her information from Mrs Maxwell. 'They built this house in 1880, I think it was.'

Daniel made a teasing face at her.

'Then they should have been ashamed of themselves. It's gruesome,' he said.

Kit and Laura didn't dispute this. The damp stucco façade, balustraded roof and ornamental chimneys of Maddimoss House didn't appeal to them, either.

'You should see the inside,' said Kit.

Daniel laughed, pushed back his chair, and

stretched out his long legs to the stove. He seemed more cheerful now that he was warm and fed.

'Well, it can't be helped. I'll have to think again,' he said. 'Meanwhile, I might stick around here for a bit. See the sights, you know. I've got plenty of time.'

Kit looked at him, puzzled. She had been wondering how old he was, and reckoned he was probably fifteen. She had assumed he was on his half-term holiday.

'Shouldn't you be at school?' she inquired.

The answer was very cool.

'No way. I've left. I was thrown out, actually.'

Kit gasped.

'You mean – expelled?'

It was a word she knew from reading stories about girls' boarding schools, which had once belonged to Laura's mother.

'Yip,' confirmed Daniel perkily. Then as he saw Kit's shocked face, his lips began to twitch. A gleam of mischief appeared in his eyes. 'Do you want to hear my terrible tale?' he asked her.

Kit nodded, wide-eyed.

'Well, then,' Daniel said. 'On the last night of term, before the summer holidays, one of the boys – well, me, actually – brought in a few cans of beer for a little celebration. Against the rules, of course. Then around midnight somebody – me again, probably – had the bright idea of taking a dip in the fountain outside the headmaster's house. Unfortunately old Whiskers didn't see the funny side. Something to do with the rude song we were singing, probably. He wasn't musical.'

'So he expelled you,' said Kit, uncertain whether to laugh or not. 'What on earth did your mum say?'

Daniel burst out laughing.

'Oh, Mum was OK,' he said. 'Normal high spirits, she said, and she'd never liked Whiskers anyway. It was my dad who freaked out. He's a doctor in Birmingham, and he did his nut about the money he'd spent on my education, and how I'd had life far too easy, unlike himself, and how he wasn't going to fork out any more cash to keep a drunken lout with an earring. God, he was boring. Then when I said I didn't want to be a doctor, he went into orbit.' Daniel swallowed some more coffee, and went on, 'Anyway, he calmed down eventually, and since I was sixteen and didn't have to go to school, Mum persuaded him to let me come away by myself for a few months – she said to sort myself out. I've been working since August for a friend of hers who has a hotel in Aberdeen. Now I'm on my way home, hitching lifts and looking for someone called Maddimoss. But I don't have to be back in Birmingham till Easter. That's when I've got to turn up and tell Dad what I'm going to do with the rest of my life.'

'Do you know?' asked Laura, who had listened impassively to Daniel's story.

The boy shook his head. Mirth had gone out of him.

'Dad's really keen for me to be a doctor,' he said, 'so that I can take over when he retires. He's fifty-eight, which is old to have a son my age, and I'm an only child, so it really matters to him. And even if he is always bugging me about my earring, and banging on about the youth of today, he's a nice old dad, and I'd like to please him. Only I don't like blood, and I'd rather be an artist. Art's the only thing I'm interested in.'

'Laura's an artist,' Kit said.

Daniel looked up at her, but Laura shook her head.

'Not any more,' she said. 'I taught art before I had children, but I haven't painted for a long time.'

There was the kind of silence that follows a story not completely told. Some unspoken sadness cooled the air. Daniel stood up, and reached for his jacket.

'I'd better push off now,' he said. 'Thanks for feeding me.'

That was when Kit noticed he didn't have any luggage.

'But where are you going?' she asked anxiously. 'And where are your things?'

'I left my rucksack at the youth hostel at Tillyrie,' said Daniel, as he struggled into his unpleasantly wet jacket. 'I've booked in for two nights. Tomorrow I'll probably look around, and see if I can find a job for a few weeks. If not, I'll move on.'

Suddenly it mattered more than anything else to Kit that Daniel shouldn't move on.

'Laura,' she began, then stopped herself.

She knew that Laura might disapprove of a boy expelled for getting drunk at boarding school. Having fed Daniel, she might think she'd done enough. The days when Laura was always doing favours for people were in the past. Still, Kit crossed her fingers tightly under the table, and willed Laura with all her strength not to let Daniel go. Perhaps it worked.

'Hang on a minute,' Laura said, glancing at the wet black window-panes. 'You can't walk back to Tillyrie in weather like this. It's five miles, for heaven's sake. Besides –' Kit held her breath '– you can stay here, if you like. There's a bedroom we don't use, and I don't imagine it would bother Miss Sorley.'

Daniel stared at her incredulously.

'But – don't you mind – what happened at the school?' he stammered, embarrassed for the first time. 'I wouldn't have told you if I hadn't thought –'

'That you'd never see us again,' Laura finished for him. Her unforced smile was beautiful. 'Let's just say I agree with your mum.'

'And Mr Maxwell would give you a job, I think,' said Kit, remembering. 'I heard him say last week that he was looking for extra hands.'

'My lucky day,' said Daniel, smiling as he unzipped his jacket.

# 7

# The Bronze
# Bell

'When I come home,' Kit told Daniel, as she checked her school bag on Monday morning, 'I'm going to show you something brilliant. Awesome, actually.'

She felt she could hardly wait to take her new friend to the Japanese garden. But the response wasn't enthusiastic. Daniel, who was groping around the kitchen in his pyjamas and a pair of grey suede moccasins, yawned cavernously.

'Great,' he mumbled. 'Where does Laura keep the marmalade?'

Obviously he wasn't what Peter called 'a morning person'. But Kit wasn't put out. She was in high spirits, and she didn't believe that anyone could resist the garden's spell. Least of all Daniel, who thought that a Japanese flower print in the hall was one of the most beautiful pictures he had ever seen. Kit hadn't even noticed it.

The second half of Sunday had been the happiest time Kit had experienced since Juliet died. In the early evening, Laura had taken Daniel in the car to Tillyrie, to fetch his rucksack. When they came back, she had insisted that he 'phone his parents, and tell them where he was.

'It's me, Dad. Dandy-doo, thanks. How's yourself? You'll never believe this . . .'

Then there had been the fun of installing Daniel in the tiny bedroom beside the front door. The disappearing Japanese temporarily forgotten, Kit had run busily to and fro, fetching an electric blanket to air the bed, looking in the hall cupboard for a heater, bringing Daniel some posters to brighten up the dingy walls. After supper, Laura had 'phoned Mr Maxwell, who said that if Daniel came by in the morning, he'd see what could be arranged. Kit had gone to bed late, and slept dreamlessly.

The day in school seemed longer than usual, but then Kit had never before been in a hurry to get home. Through the classroom window she kept an anxious eye on the weather, but the sleet-turning-to-snow predicted by the weather forecaster on Sunday night didn't happen. The wind sank, exhausted, during the morning, and by afternoon it was another ordinary February day. Kit was relieved. She knew that the garden under snow would be stunning, but a heavy fall would add another, probably insuperable hazard to the way through the wood.

When Kit got home at last, Daniel was in the kitchen, drinking coffee with Laura who, Kit thought unkindly, looked just as scruffy but slightly less dead than usual. It seemed she too liked having Daniel there. Daniel winked at Kit, and gave her the 'thumbs up' sign.

'It's all arranged,' he told her jubilantly. 'Mr Maxwell is taking me on part-time as an orra-lad.'

'A what?'

'An orra-lad. It means I'll be doing odd jobs,

whatever needs doing that day. I've to work eight to one, and Mrs Maxwell will give me a meal before I knock off. I start tomorrow.'

'What did Mr Maxwell say about your earring?' Kit couldn't resist asking.

'He said his bull had one. Through its nose,' said Daniel cheerfully. 'Now come on. What were you going to show me?'

As she walked up the farm road with Daniel, Kit was bouncing with eagerness. Having someone to share the Japanese garden with was a pleasure she had not expected. She had wondered briefly, on the bus, whether she should also tell Daniel about the strange photograph, but had decided not to risk it. She knew how humiliated she would feel if he laughed, although she was honest enough to admit that two days ago she would certainly have laughed herself.

'We go through the wood here,' she said, when they reached the fork in the road. 'It's very brambly, but it's worth it at the other end.'

'If you say so,' said Daniel dubiously, peering into the dark entrance. But he followed her without a fuss.

Ever since Friday, Kit had been carrying in her head a picture of the Japanese garden as she had seen it then. Foolishly, as she now stumbled through the wood with Daniel laughing and cursing at her heels, she was imagining that he would see the same golden, sunset scene. So she was cross with herself, and disappointed, when she saw plain grey daylight among the trees. How stupid, she thought, not to realize that, of course, Daniel's first impression would be completely different.

But there was no need to worry. Although the sky was like grey suede, and the garden's colours had faded to fawn, olive and pale green, it was just as enchanting. And when Kit glanced at Daniel, she saw the expression on his face which she knew must have been on hers, when first she stood here. The magic of the garden was reflected in his eyes, but he didn't know what to say.

'Ace, isn't it?' ventured Kit, but when Daniel didn't answer, she didn't press the question.

Abruptly Daniel went off to the left, along a path that disappeared into a thicket of rhododendron. Although Kit had been hoping to walk round the lake with him, she didn't follow. She wasn't pushy, and she could understand that he might prefer to look at the garden alone. She watched him emerge from the rhododendrons and walk along the water's edge. If she went in the opposite direction, she thought, she could keep him in view, and meet up with him half-way round.

So Kit went off up the other side of the lake, but she had only gone a little way when she was diverted. On her right, she saw a little path of mossy stepping-stones. They invited feet, and somehow Kit's feet found them irresistible. Passing under a shiny wooden gateway with gently curving crossbar, she followed the path away from the lake. Beyond a stone lantern, shaped like the king on a chessboard, she found herself in front of a little hut among the pines. Kit noticed that on one side there was a tall stone, almost entirely covered with moss, and on the other a bell, hanging from the bough of a pine tree. But for the moment, she was interested in the hut itself.

It was set on a platform, with steps, and a railing all round. It had no doors, and when she peered in between two panels of lattice, Kit saw that the interior was full of decayed leaves, layer upon blackened layer, piled high by winds of many years. The smell was acrid, and when she noticed that the space between the leaves and the roof was strung with lacy grey cobwebs, she had no wish to linger. Shivering at the thought of unseen spiders, she hurried back down the steps, and went to look at the bell.

Balancing on a rusty hook driven into the pine branch, the bell was a huge version, about twenty-five centimetres across, of the jingle-bell on a baby's rattle. Kit saw that it was made of bronze, disfigured by a rash of green verdigris, and that from its slit mouth a dirty rope hung down to the ground. Without pausing to think, she took hold of the rope, and pulled. A split second later she was falling on her knees, stuffing her fingers frantically into her ears, trying to protect her brain from the appalling noise she had caused.

Never in her life had Kit heard such a noise. As the hidden clapper touched the inside of the bell, a pure, sweet note sounded. Then it broke and changed into an intolerable thrumming which got louder and louder, until its vibrations shook the sleeping garden, and roused rooks in resentful flurries from the trees. Simultaneously a low, chill wind stirred the grass. But it wasn't until the nerve-jangling sound had flattened itself on the wood, and silence returned, that panic gripped Kit. Something had happened. The silence wasn't the same.

Then she knew. No one was visible, but someone

had come. He was hiding behind the mossy stone on the other side of the hut. For a dreadful, long moment Kit was too frightened to move, then she was too frightened not to. Sweating with fear, she stumbled down the stepping-stones, and ran blindly along the edge of the lake. She didn't know where she was going, only that she had to get away. At last, through what felt like a swarm of bees buzzing round her head, she heard Daniel's voice.

'Kit, where are you? Puss! Oh, there you are. What in hell was that noise?'

Kit heard his running footsteps, then he was in front of her on the path. Strong hands grabbed her shoulders, and held her. Swimmily she saw Daniel's pale, startled face. Taking a great gulp of air, she tried to explain.

'A bell,' she gasped. 'Hanging on a tree. I rang a bell.'

She was going to say more, but a splutter of amusement stopped her. She could feel Daniel's laughter right down his arms.

'Jeeze!' he hooted. 'Was that all? I thought a spacecraft had landed!'

Kit saw his grey eyes twinkling, inviting her to think it funny too. But she was not in the mood. Hurt and angry, she shook off Daniel's hands, and pulled away from him.

'Get lost,' she growled. 'I'm going home.'

# 8

# Evening

For Kit, it was a wonderful occasion ruined. Daniel let her go, and she had to struggle back alone, her spine rigid with terror as she imagined someone, silent and invisible, stalking her through the wood. She didn't dare to glance behind, and with pounding heart and fear-weakened legs she thought she would never reach the road. As the garden fell away behind her, however, the sense of a ghostly presence faded; Kit knew that whoever had come at the sound of the bell hadn't followed her into the wood. She had a fleeting experience of relief, before more rational feelings overwhelmed her. Sick with loneliness and disappointment she ran desolately home, shut her bedroom door and wept bitterly.

Daniel came back at five. Kit saw him pass her bedroom window in the dusk, and heard him whistling as he crossed the hall. She stayed in her room until seven, then sulked through supper. Annoyingly, neither Laura nor Daniel seemed to notice. They ate the Chicken Maryland which Laura, amazingly, had stirred herself to cook, and each had a glass of wine, which Kit wasn't yet allowed. They talked about painting.

'You know Van Gogh's painting of irises? So like

that flower print in the hall. Japan must have been an influence, don't you think?'

'I hadn't thought of it, but yes. Dad took me to the Van Gogh museum in Amsterdam . . .'

Kit, who knew nothing about art, felt childish and left out. Seeing Laura once again neglecting her for someone else aroused old resentments, and although in her heart she knew that Laura too was lonely and in need of friendship, she refused to care. The day which had begun so brightly was ending in misery, and Kit could scarcely hold back her tears. The minute supper was over, she took her bitter thoughts off to the bath. She was in bed, grimly trying to finish her maths homework, when she heard a knock, and Daniel stuck his brown head round the door.

'Am I allowed in?' he asked.

'If you like,' replied Kit suspiciously, not knowing whether to be pleased or not.

Daniel brought the rest of his body into the room, and stood on the faded carpet with his hands in his pockets. His legs were growing too long for his trousers, and as she looked at his bare feet in his furry grey moccasins, something ached in Kit. She had always wanted a big brother instead of Juliet, and Daniel – even if he did tease her by calling her 'Puss', and even if she fell out with him every day – was the big brother she'd give anything to have. Daniel sat down on the end of Kit's bed, and looked around the square, high-ceilinged room.

'I know it's awful,' said Kit defensively.

But Daniel said, 'No. I can see it was awful to start with, but it's nice now. You've done all you could.'

This was true. Kit had pinned up posters of Spain on the discoloured walls, and set out her collection of costume dolls. She had filled a shelf with books borrowed from other parts of the house, and found lamps for her desk and bedside table. It was awful, just the same. The only really attractive thing was the silk shawl, which she had suspended from thumb-tacks above her desk, where the lamp lit it pinkly from below.

'That's nice,' said Daniel appreciatively.

Kit sat up in bed and hugged her knees.

'I found it in a drawer in the sitting-room,' she said, and couldn't resist going on to tell Daniel about the other baby clothes, and Miss Sorley being a foundling, long ago. 'I wondered if the shawl belonged to her,' she concluded.

But she could see that this story wasn't grasping Daniel's attention. It would have been different if Miss Sorley's name had been Maddimoss.

'I wondered about those letters, Y A N A G I,' said Kit, spelling them out in a last effort. 'What d'you suppose they mean?'

'I haven't a clue,' replied Daniel flatly. Then, changing the subject, he went on, 'Listen, Puss. This afternoon – I'm sorry I laughed. I wasn't making a fool of you. I got a hell of a fright, and I didn't realize you'd got a worse one.'

It was a handsome apology.

Kit muttered, 'That's OK,' hoping she didn't look as ridiculously pleased as she felt.

Just for a moment, she was tempted to pick up the implied question, and tell Daniel the truth about the fright she'd had. But she didn't. It was like the business of the photograph, impossible to explain, impossible to share. Anyway, Daniel didn't probe further. He seemed to have something else on his mind.

'Puss, I've been thinking,' he said. 'We really should do something about that garden.'

'Should we?' Kit frowned, not understanding. 'Like what?'

'Clean up the mess,' Daniel explained. 'Weed the paths. Unblock the waterfalls. Later on, if I can get some wood, and borrow tools, we might have a go at mending the shrines – tea houses, whatever they are.'

Just for a moment, outrage re-ignited the anger in Kit's head. Damn it, she thought. It was her garden. She had found it, and if it hadn't been for her, Daniel would never even have known it existed. Yet here he was already, acting the boss, telling her what they ought to do. But when she saw the eager, friendly expression on his face, her indignation faded as quickly as it had come. She was being unfair. She had chosen to share her secret with him, after all.

'I could work there in the afternoons,' urged Daniel, quite unaware that he had given offence. 'You could give me a hand when you come home from school. If you like, that is,' he added uncertainly, as Kit failed to respond.

Kit remained silent, as a terrible struggle took place in her mind. As her unspoken fury evaporated, the memory of that afternoon's terror took its place; she remembered how she had sworn, as she ran whimpering home, that she would never go near the Japanese garden again. The very idea made her quail. But at the same time she realized just how much she

55

did want to work with Daniel in the garden – and what the consequences would be if she turned his suggestion down. Daniel would get up and say, 'Well, never mind,' and the friendship Kit longed for would never recover from the blow. He would carry out his plan without her, and she would be eaten up by frustration and jealousy as she watched her garden becoming his. For a moment, fear and desire nearly tore Kit apart.

But then she remembered that on Friday she had needed all her courage to enter the garden at all. Surely, with so much at stake, she could now be brave enough to enter it again? She would be with Daniel, this time. Kit took a deep breath, and made up her mind.

'I do like,' she said resolutely. 'Only –'

'Only what?'

'I just wondered why.'

Daniel shrugged, and made a circular movement with his thin hands.

'It's hard to explain,' he admitted. 'After you'd gone, I walked around a bit, just looking, and listening to the silence. It isn't like anywhere else, is it? And it needs help. Otherwise it will die.'

On an impulse, Kit flipped her Maths book shut, and reached for her dressing-gown.

'Come with me a minute,' she said. 'I want to show you something.' Doing up her buttons as she went, she led Daniel across the hall to the sitting-room. 'Look at this,' she added, pushing open the heavy varnished door.

In the thin electric light, Daniel peered in fascination at the picture of Mr and Mrs Sorley in their

Japanese garden. And so did Kit, because behind the Sorleys, on a little bridge, was someone who had been absent since Saturday.

'There's a Japanese,' said Daniel, astonished.

'The gardener,' Kit managed to say.

Kit and Daniel gazed at the Japanese gardener, and he gazed back at them. Then, very slowly, he began to fade. It took quite a while for his features to blur, and even longer for the shadow he became to pale, disintegrate, and finally disappear.

# 9

# A Gentle
# Spirit

'He's buried in Frankly churchyard,' Kit said.

It was very late, and they were still in her room, drinking hot chocolate she had made and talking about the Japanese gardener. Kit had, after all, found it very easy to tell Daniel about her strange experiences. For one thing, he had now seen the photograph's odd behaviour for himself. For another, he already believed in ghosts.

'Not that I've ever seen anything spooky myself, until now,' he said, 'but my granny saw a ghost once, in London. In Hyde Park, I think it was. A friend came to tell her he was dead. She was a very calm person, and truthful. If she said it happened, then it really did.'

'So you reckon what we saw tonight was a ghost?' asked Kit, thankful that she could now use the word 'we'.

Daniel nodded.

'Has to be,' he replied.

'And what I felt in the garden this afternoon?'

Kit watched Daniel considering this question before he answered it. Eventually he said, 'I can't be completely sure, because I didn't feel it myself. But the garden's such an extraordinary place, it isn't difficult to believe there's a spirit there. So yes. I reckon if a ghost can appear in a photograph of a garden, he can be there too.'

Upstairs, Miss Sorley's clock struck eleven, its clear, unhurried notes measuring the pause during which they thought about this enormous possibility. It was Kit who broke the silence.

'Daniel, are you scared?'

Daniel twiddled his earring, and considered this.

Then he said firmly, 'No. I know what's happening is very weird, but I can't believe anything to do with that garden is evil. Besides, that Japanese guy has a nice face. I reckon he's a gentle spirit.' He noticed the sceptical look in Kit's eyes, and grinned sympathetically. 'I know you got a hell of a fright this afternoon,' he added, 'but I'm sure I'm right. There's no reason to suppose that ghosts only want to frighten us.'

'Isn't there?'

'No. Why would they want to scare people they don't even know?' urged Daniel. 'Isn't it far more likely they're trying to tell us something – or even asking us for help?'

'So you think that's what he's doing?' asked Kit.

She admired Daniel's cool, and was doing her best to match it.

'Seems probable.'

'Then it's also probable we'll see him again,' said Kit, just managing not to scream, and dive under the bedclothes.

'Sure,' nodded Daniel. 'Though not in the photograph, next time. I reckon he just used that to draw himself to our attention. I think he'll show up in the garden one day – when it suits his purpose.'

If anyone had told her on Friday, Kit thought, that by Monday she'd be taking such a bizarre suggestion seriously, she'd have thought they were cracked. But she was now taking it very seriously indeed.

'Daniel,' she said, 'why do you suppose he's chosen to get in touch with us?'

Daniel gave her a startled look, then said, 'Oh, come on, Puss. There's no way of knowing that. Does there have to be a reason?'

Kit thought that there did. But she was tired, and didn't press the question. Daniel stretched, got to his feet and yawned widely.

'It would be nice if we knew his name,' he said.

Which was when Kit said, 'He's buried in Frankly churchyard.'

Tuesday was a still, tender day, sunless but with a hint of spring in the air. Just a hint, however. By half-past three, when Kit got off the bus at Frankly crossroads, it was bitterly cold, with coils of mist unravelling up the Carse from the river, and the edges of puddles crisp with forming crystals of ice. As arranged, Daniel was waiting for her, and they walked up the village street together, past the post office and the Sorley Arms inn. Frankly church was ahead of them, riding the hill like a grey ship on a billow of winter grass. With a little shiver that had nothing to do with the chilly air, Kit pushed open the stiff iron gate and stepped into the stone-walled churchyard.

'Mrs Maxwell says the grave's down in the corner, behind the Sorleys' tomb,' she said, pausing to look around. Then 'That'll be it, won't it?' she added, pointing down the hill to the left of the gate.

Daniel nodded, and strode away on his long legs. Kit had to run to keep up as he zig-zagged through the old grey headstones, down towards a large white marble memorial. Unlike anything else in this quiet, unassuming place, it was fenced with high, rusty black railings and overhung by gloomy grey trees.

'Yuk,' said Daniel, making a face at a vast carved angel, moss-blinded and with greenish lichen feathering his wings.

Kit agreed, but she couldn't help being interested. Peering through the railings, she read the fading names of Sorleys dead and forgotten long ago. *Here lie the mortal remains of Euphan Sorley of Maddimoss and his wife Rebecca . . . their daughter Jane . . . Captain George Sorley . . . His wife Lady Judith Vane.* The last Sorleys to be buried in this damp, depressing place were the couple who had made the Japanese garden, *John Sorley, traveller, who died 3 July 1940 aged 67 years, also his wife Hester Methven who died 12 February 1953 aged 78 years.* Kit memorized their names and dates, not knowing why.

'Oi!' Daniel, who hadn't given more than a withering glance to the Sorleys' memorial, stuck out his brown head from behind the railings. 'Stop wasting time on that rotten lot. Come round here.'

Startled by the tone of his voice, Kit hurried to join him. She found him standing in front of four small, plain gravestones with their backs to the churchyard wall. She was even more surprised to see anger in his eyes, and a flush on his usually pale cheeks.

61

'What's up?' demanded Kit, wondering what could possibly have upset him.

Daniel kicked at the grass with a booted foot.

'It's these ruddy Sorleys,' he growled. 'I don't rate people like them. They stick up great ugly monuments to themselves, but when it comes to the people who work for them – I mean, look at this.' He jabbed his forefinger at the line of stones. '"Jenny Cameron, nurse to Judith and Clare Sorley." Big deal. "Frank Carter, coachman." "Lachlan Scott, butler." You'd think they only existed to serve the Sorleys.' Kit couldn't think why he was in such a bad mood about something that didn't affect him personally, but she said nothing, and found out. 'My grandad was a butler,' Daniel informed her, 'to some old geezer called Lord Pinkerton. He called Grandad "Garth", but Grandad had to call him "My lord".'

'Did your grandad mind?' asked Kit.

'No, but I do,' muttered Daniel sullenly.

'What about your granny?'

Kit remembered that Daniel's granny had gone to London to be a maid. In spite of himself, Daniel grinned.

'Oh, her. She just thought posh folk were a big laugh,' he said. But then his face went sour again as he pointed to the last stone in the row. It was slightly apart from the others, and sheltered by the angle of the wall. 'Look at that,' he snorted. 'The man comes thousands of miles to work in their garden, and they can't even put his full name on his grave.'

Kit found herself wishing he'd shut up. All this ranting and raging had almost made her forget what they'd come here to see. Quietly she stepped over the frosted grass, and in the late afternoon light read the words, *Kojima, gardener, 1895–1930*. So he had been dead for two years when Mr and Mrs Sorley were photographed in their Japanese garden. Kit felt awed, but not, after all that had happened, surprised. Then she noticed something else, mysterious in a different way. The rest of the small sandstone tablets were as neglected and disfigured as the grotesque monument which towered over them. But Kojima's was not. Snowdrops shone around it in the grass, and at its foot stood a simple black vase. In it, elegantly arranged, were a twig with red berries, a sprig of winter jasmine and a single Christmas rose.

'Someone remembers him,' Kit said softly.

They walked home in the misty twilight along the old railway line, passing the wood which sheltered the Japanese garden, and the field where the Crawfords' new house stood roofless in a sea of mud. Daniel was still grousing about not knowing the gardener's forename, but Kit was more interested in the mysterious winter flowers.

'Do you suppose Kojima was married, and some of his descendants still live nearby?' she wondered. 'They might take flowers to his grave.'

Daniel thought this was unlikely.

'Mrs Maxwell would have mentioned if there were still Japanese people at Maddimoss,' he said. 'I think it's more likely a relation of his is visiting Scotland from Japan. A student, say. Told by his parents to visit Uncle Kojima's grave. Japanese people respect their ancestors, I think.'

Kit supposed this explanation was better than hers, though it didn't convince her completely either.

The one thing she was sure of was that the flowers had been arranged by someone Japanese. She had seen the garish, blowsy bouquets decorating other graves, and she didn't believe any Scot could have made something so perfect out of two twigs and a flower.

Daniel was silent for the last quarter-mile, amusing himself by tickling the leafless hedges with a long stick, making the shrivelled berries dance. As they came out on to the farm road below Whitewells, he said, 'Puss, I want to ask you something.'

'Feel free,' invited Kit.

'I was wondering,' Daniel said. 'The day I arrived, Laura said she used to teach art before she had children. Does Laura have another child?'

Briefly, Kit told him about Laura's other child. It was too dark to see his face now, but she could sense his horror.

'God, that was rotten,' he said. 'I'd no idea. You didn't mind me asking, did you?'

'Not at all,' Kit assured him.

She was in her bedroom, changing into her slippers, when it occurred to her that she hadn't thought about Juliet since Sunday. She hadn't dreamed about her either.

# 10

# Hester Sorley's
## Book

The rest of the week passed quietly, without anything happening to shed light on the mysteries which seemed to have woven themselves around Maddimoss. Kojima didn't show up again in the photograph. Daniel's scouring of directories and reference books for entries under 'Maddimoss' brought him no success. The letters embroidered on the silk shawl remained cryptic. As for the flowers on Kojima's grave, Kit couldn't think of any explanation more likely than the ones she and Daniel had concocted as they walked back from Frankly. Occasionally she wondered whether any of the mysteries were connected, but of course there was no way of knowing that either.

Meanwhile, despite having had to change her mind about ghosts, and knowing that the time was approaching when she would have to go into the Japanese garden again, Kit was happy, in some ways happier than she had ever been. She loved having Daniel around, and every school day was now a matter of getting through the hours until she could rush home, change into old clothes and dash to meet him out of doors.

Despite his disappointment over his fruitless search

for someone called Maddimoss, Daniel was exuberant, and pleased with everything. Although he was
having to work hard whitewashing the milking shed
and mending fences for Mr Maxwell, he had plenty
of energy left for the rest of the day. The first task,
he said, was to clear the path through the wood, so
that they could get in and out of the garden easily.
With tools borrowed from Mr Maxwell, he spent the
afternoons sawing and chopping till sweat ran down
his face, while Kit stacked the cut branches under
the trees.

As they got closer to the garden, Kit couldn't help
remembering her fright, and feeling uneasy; she was
by no means as positive as Daniel that the Japanese
gardener meant them no harm. Yet she didn't for a
moment regret the promise she had made to help.
Mixed in with her fear she found other feelings,
curiosity, loyalty to Daniel, and a strange, strong
belief that she was in some way facing a test which
she had to pass. She summoned courage by telling
herself that she would stick close to Daniel, and keep
well away from the hut among the pines.

On Saturday, Kit and Daniel both had lunch at
Whitewells Farm, and got from Mrs Maxwell the
assurance that Kojima had been unmarried, and
that no other Japanese people had ever lived at
Maddimoss. Afterwards, in the mild, thinly sunny
afternoon, they walked round the Japanese garden
together, noting down jobs that needed to be done.
Kit felt nervous as they emerged from the wood, but
nothing happened to alarm her, and soon she was
soothed by the tranquil enchantment of the place.

'It would take months and months to restore it

properly,' said Daniel regretfully, 'and I've only got six weeks. But never mind, Puss. We'll do what we can, starting tomorrow morning at nine. Don't be late!'

The cheek of this almost took Kit's breath away. Getting Daniel to Whitewells by eight o'clock in the morning had proved a Herculean task, and it was only thanks to Kit's banging on his door and making him breakfast that he was on his way up the hill at two minutes to eight, eating a bacon sandwich as he ran.

'I've always thought I'd like to push somebody in a lake,' she said. 'So just watch it, Skinny.'

In the hilarious chase through the wood that followed, Kit forgot something else she had intended to say. It came back to her when they were at supper, sitting at the stove end of the huge table where the Sorleys' servants had eaten their meals long ago.

'Daniel,' she said. 'Do you suppose we should mention to Miss Sorley that we're going to work in the Japanese garden? It does belong to her, after all.'

Knowing Daniel's poor opinion of the Sorley family, she half expected him to pooh-pooh this suggestion. But he nodded agreeably.

'Yip. Could do,' he said, twirling spaghetti on his fork and stuffing it messily into his mouth. 'She should be ruddy grateful if you ask me. I'll go and chat her up after supper.'

But Laura, who had been told about the garden project by Daniel, shook her head cautiously.

'I wouldn't do that if I were you,' she said.

'I just thought it would be polite,' said Kit, feeling miffed.

Honestly, she thought, grown-ups were impossible to please. Laura looked apologetic.

'Yes, I know,' she said, 'and of course it would be the right thing to do – if Miss Sorley was like other people. But she isn't, and it's my guess she'd say no. Not because she's nasty, or ungrateful, but because Daniel's appearing suddenly at her door would frighten her.'

'Am I so ugly?' demanded Daniel indignantly.

'Yes,' said Kit.

But Laura went on seriously, 'Please, listen. Miss Sorley's housekeeper, Mrs Brown, comes in here on Mondays to dust and do the hoovering. She's a nice woman, obviously fond of Miss Sorley, and not the kind to gossip about her. But she did tell me, early on, that Miss Sorley is very shy, and finds meeting strangers a severe trial. I think it was her way of warning me not to invite Miss Sorley for coffee, which I wasn't going to do. But if that's how the old lady feels, she won't take kindly to being chatted up by you. OK?'

'So, shall we just go ahead without telling her?' asked Kit.

Laura shrugged.

'Why not?' she replied. 'I don't know why you're bothering, but you're certainly not doing any harm. I don't suppose she'll ever know.'

But in this, Laura was mistaken.

Sunday was Daniel's day off, and just after nine he trundled Mr Maxwell's spare wheelbarrow along the cleared path, while Kit held steady a collection of plastic buckets, gardening gloves and borrowed tools. They found the garden eerily beautiful, with

68

ribbons of mist floating loose over the lake and the trees melting behind a vapour screen. The weather forecast was for another mild, spring-like day. Daniel, who had the plan they had made attached to a clipboard, suggested that Kit might start weeding the path along the northern shore of the lake, while he began the messy job of unblocking little stone basins, so that water could again cascade freely among the rocks.

Kit worked busily with a small fork, enjoying the earthy smell, filling a bucket with weeds and sparing the stray snowdrops and pale mauve crocuses which had invaded the path. She had no sense of any presence but Daniel's, and soon she was feeling perfectly relaxed. So it was disappointing, as well as frightening, suddenly to know that again eyes were watching her.

This time, however, the eyes were human. When Kit rather bravely stood up and looked round, she saw Miss Sorley standing on the other side of the lake, a small, round-shouldered figure in a grey tweed overcoat and black boots. With her hands in her pockets, she was watching Kit and Daniel through her dark glasses, while her black spaniel snuffled in the reeds along the lake side.

'Psst!' hissed Kit to Daniel, who was straddling the rocks above her, and filling a bucket with dark brown sludge. 'Look, across the lake! It's Miss Sorley, watching us!'

Slowly Daniel straightened his back, and turned his head. For perhaps thirty seconds, Miss Sorley stared at Kit and Daniel, and they stared at her. Then abruptly she turned on her heel, called her dog and disappeared among the rhododendrons.

'There must be another way in,' remarked Kit.

'She would know,' said Daniel indifferently, getting back to work.

'Do you suppose she'll try to stop us?' asked Kit anxiously.

'We'll soon find out,' Daniel replied.

But Miss Sorley didn't try to stop them. They worked all day in the garden, and again on Monday afternoon. When they arrived home, dirty but contented, at five o'clock, a surprise awaited them. On the kitchen table lay a book, the size of a large scrapbook, with hard blue covers.

'What's this?' inquired Kit, only the grubbiness of her fingers stopping her from opening the book.

Laura looked up from the letter she was writing on her knee by the stove.

'Mrs Brown brought it when she came down to do the hoovering,' she said. 'It's something to do with the Japanese garden. Miss Sorley thought you might like to borrow it.' Then, as Daniel whistled and Kit's eyebrows shot up in amazement, she added dryly, 'I gathered that thanks are definitely not required.'

Daniel glanced down at his filthy hands.

'I suppose we'd better shower before we look at it,' he said to Kit. 'You can go first, if you promise not to peek before I'm ready.'

'I promise,' squealed Kit, shooting out of the kitchen.

Half an hour later, washed and changed, Kit and Daniel carried Miss Sorley's book into the sitting-room, and sat down on a sofa by the fire. When Kit opened it, they saw on the first page the inscription, *The Japanese garden at Maddimoss. Hester J. Sorley, May 1912.*

'Is Miss Sorley that old?' queried Daniel in surprise.

Kit shook her head.

'I don't think it's her,' she replied. 'The old lady in the photograph was called Hester. The one who adopted Miss Sorley. Her name's on that awful tombstone we saw at Frankly.'

'Yip. That makes sense,' agreed Daniel, looking at the faded, old-fashioned writing. 'Turn over, Puss. Let's see the rest.'

Hester Sorley's book was diary, notebook and sketchbook, all in one. Between 1912 and 1930, when the last entry was made, she had put down on its cream pages everything to do with the Japanese garden. There was an account of how the duckpond had been flooded to make the lake. There were notes on the building of the huts, one a tea house, one a summer house, and one a shrine of Inari, the god who introduced rice to Japan. There were lists of plants and shrubs, plans, and lively sketches of gates, bridges and stone lanterns. The lantern at Maddimoss came from Tokyo, and was dated 1833.

'This woman was an artist,' admitted Daniel with reluctant admiration, as he examined tiny watercolours and dashing pen-and-ink sketches of wood and water.

On one page, Hester Sorley had stuck two bills paid for shipping from Japan the shrine itself and a torii.

'What's a torii?' Kit wanted to know.

Daniel pointed to another drawing, of a wooden gateway with an elegantly curving crossbar. Underneath Mrs Sorley had written, 'Torii – Inari style'.

'Of course,' exclaimed Kit. 'I remember. It's at the end of the stepping-stones, the ones that lead to the hut beside the bell.'

'I think the bell's beside the hut,' corrected Daniel. 'The hut's the important thing. It says here that the torii is at the entrance to Koraku-en, the garden of Good Fortune and Long Life. It's the most sacred part of the whole garden. It holds the shrine of Inari, a stone lantern and the sanctuary bell. The bell was brought from Miyajima in Japan, and there's also something called the Guardian Stone.'

Yes, Kit thought. That would be the mossy stone on the right of the leaf-filled hut, where someone had lurked . . . She shivered, and hastily turned the page.

Two diary entries in the book were particularly interesting. One, squeezed in between a list of shrubs and a magazine cutting on how to prune plum trees, was dated 12 August 1919.

'Kojima arrived this morning. Japanese, aged 24, from Hiroshima. No English. Family wiped out in cholera epidemic – sad tale. Accommodation: no. 3, Sparrowlea Farm Cottages. Wages: 6 shillings weekly.'

'Wow! How generous,' said Daniel sarcastically.

Kit groaned inwardly. She hoped he wasn't going to spend another hour beefing about poor servants being exploited by their rich masters, and was relieved when he said no more. Together they leafed through the remaining pages, scanning them for more references to Kojima. There was only one, the last in the book, but it was very interesting.

'20 May 1930: Have again reprimanded Kojima for neglecting his duties. Spends hours carving in the shrine of Inari.'

'Carving?' said Kit, raising her eyebrows. 'That's funny. What on earth would he be carving?'

Daniel didn't speculate, but he closed the book with a very satisfied smile.

'Puss,' he said, 'I think it's high time we investigated the shrine of Inari.'

# 11

# Koraku-en

Kit was not at all sure that she wanted to investigate the shrine of Inari. Koraku-en, the sacred place among the pines, was the one part of the garden from which she had been determined to keep away. All the next day in school, the memory of her fright there washed over her, making her hot and cold by turns. She was sorely tempted to go home, complain to Laura of a tummy-ache, and be sent to lie down with a hot-water bottle.

On the bus, however, the curiosity which had first led her into the garden once more got the better of her. She was sure that Hester Sorley's book had at last thrown up a clue, and she was dying to know whether Daniel had found anything exciting. So Kit again found a kind of courage, which carried her through the wood, under the torii and up the path of stepping-stones. She found Daniel sitting peacefully on the steps of the shrine. Beside him was a vast pile of decayed leaves, with a spade driven into its crown.

'Yoo-hoo,' Daniel greeted her. 'Nice compost, eh?'

'You're beginning to sound like Mr Maxwell,' warned Kit, wrinkling her nose and giving a wide berth both to the reeking pile and the bronze bell.

She sat down beside Daniel, and looked cautiously around her at the stone lantern, the Guardian Stone and the encircling trees. Koraku-en was thickly wrapped in silence. There was no birdsong, no breath of wind to rustle the branches, or stir the rope which hung from the sanctuary bell. Just for a moment, Kit had the sense of a place waiting for something to happen, but she was wise enough to understand that the feeling was probably inside herself.

'Found anything?' she asked.

'Come and see.'

Daniel got to his feet and went up into the shrine. Kit followed him, suddenly more wary of spiders than of apparitions. But she saw at once that the cobwebs, as well as the leaves, had been cleared away. Only the fusty smell remained.

As her eyes adjusted to the dimness, Kit saw that inside the shrine was small, about two metres square, with a steeply pointed roof. The back and side walls were solid, but the door space, between two latticed panels, let in enough light to see by. Along the back wall ran a shelf, and Kit was amused to see two wooden foxes sitting on it. They were black with damp, and had faint, furry moss on their backs, but they faced each other perkily with pricked ears and upright tails. Quaintly, they were wearing bibs, still flecked with flakes of red paint.

'They were on the floor, under the leaves,' said Daniel. 'We'll take them home and clean them up. Now see what else I found.'

From inside his jacket he withdrew a small, grimy wooden board, with a hole at the top for hanging it on a nail. When Kit took it to the doorway to examine it in a better light, she saw that on one side it had a faded silhouette of a prancing horse. When she turned it over, she saw that there was some curvy Japanese writing on the other.

いまめのまめの願いは
幼き娘の竹末に
神の御加護
あらんことのみ

'I wonder if it's a message?' she said, mysteriously thrilled.

'Yes. So do I,' agreed Daniel. 'It was hanging on the wall, behind the cobwebs.'

Thoughtfully Kit wiped away some of the dirt with a paper handkerchief.

'The only thing is, it isn't carved,' she pointed out.

'Come back in,' invited Daniel. 'There's something else.'

Kit slipped the little board into her coat pocket, and turned round. She saw Daniel squatting down, facing the back wall of the shrine. She went and crouched beside him, and following his pointing forefinger, saw what she had longed to see. Deeply carved into the wall, below the shelf, were five vertical lines of Japanese characters, jet black against the damp, discoloured wood.

立別れ
いなばの山の
峯に生ふる
まつとしきかば
今かへりこむ

Kit was silent as she ran her fingers over the carved shapes, tracing their beautiful, mystifying lines and curves. Then she sat back on her heels and shook her head.

'Oh, dear,' she sighed. 'I wonder what it all means?'

'We must try to find out,' said Daniel, with a note of urgency in his voice. 'I have a strange feeling that it's very important, though I don't know why.'

Kit agreed – and so, it appeared, did someone else.

He was there when they came out of the shrine, a pale, twilit figure standing motionless in the middle of Koraku-en. He was grey, and slightly translucent against the solid background of the trees, yet all of him, from his thick, gleaming hair to his slender feet in straw sandals, was clearly defined. Kit had known for more than a week that she might encounter Kojima in the garden, but no amount of imagining a ghostly confrontation could have prepared her for the shock of actually seeing him. She began to shake and sweat, her chest tightened, and for a sickening moment she thought she would go mad with terror.

But then she felt Daniel's fingers gripping her shoulder, and it steadied her to remember that she wasn't alone. Glancing up, she saw an interest on Daniel's face so intense that there was no room for fear, and that helped her too. Clutching one of the foxes to her pounding chest, she flicked her eyes back to the apparition. The shy eyes she knew so well from the photograph smiled at her, and with a great rush of relief she realized that Daniel had been right. This ghost didn't want to frighten her. It even came into her mind that he had hidden behind the Guardian Stone last time, when he saw how afraid she was. She smiled back at him, and began to breathe normally again.

Kojima stood still for a few moments, as if he wanted to give them time to get used to him. Then he glided forward and stood on the moss at the bottom of the steps. No words were spoken, but some current of understanding passed between them. Gratitude and encouragement flowed from Kojima. His young face shone with pleasure as he pointed to the wooden board sticking out of Kit's pocket, and he nodded eagerly in the direction of the shrine. Then he bowed, and, quite naturally, Daniel and Kit bowed back. When they straightened up, he was gone.

# 12

# An Exchange
## of Notes

'I don't say,' remarked Kit, 'that I'd never be afraid of a ghost again. I still think lots of ghosts could be pretty terrifying. But I'll never be afraid of that one. He's OK.'

It was after supper, and she and Daniel were sitting at the table, using cocktail sticks to pick dirt out of the foxes' ears and tails. Laura was out of the room, switching on their electric blankets. Daniel wiped the end of his stick on his trousers, and nodded gravely.

'Yes,' he said. 'I reckon what happened today proves what we thought, that he contacted us because he wants us to help him. And since he's so delighted that we've found the board, it must have a message on it. Something that matters a lot to him.'

'After sixty-odd years?' wondered Kit.

'I don't suppose he's stuck around the garden all this time for nothing,' Daniel said.

Laura came back just then, so talk of Kojima had to stop. But Kit thought over what Daniel had said, and concluded that it made a lot of sense.

Laura had been unexpectedly excited by the discovery of the foxes. Now she sat down at the table, and looked at them closely.

'You should let them dry out naturally,' she said, 'then treat them with fungicide to stop the mould growing again. After that they'll need a couple of coats of wood preservative. I wouldn't half like to repaint them,' she added longingly, examining the faded red bibs and traces of gold on the foxes' ears, noses and paws.

'Do it then. You're an artist,' Daniel coaxed her. 'We can get paint at the do-it-yourself shop in Tillyrie.'

He had never mentioned the tragedy of Juliet's death to Laura, but Kit had noticed that, since he found out, he had been quietly kind and helpful to her. Kit, who thought less about Juliet these days, sometimes wondered if Laura thought less about her too. But she suspected not. Since Daniel came, Laura had smiled more, but the smile never touched her eyes.

However, 'I'll go and buy the paint tomorrow,' Laura said, with an eagerness which Kit supposed must be a good sign – then had to remind herself hastily that Laura wasn't her mother, and she didn't really care.

'I'm going to restore that shrine,' Daniel told Laura. 'I'm going to scrub it down and put on wood preservative, and mend the railings and the roof. I love the place.'

'Mrs Maxwell tells me it's haunted,' said Laura teasingly. 'The ghost's an old woman in a long black cloak. So you'd better watch out, that's all.'

'Awesome,' murmured Daniel, avoiding Kit's eye.

'Listen,' said Kit, who was kneeling on a chair with Hester Sorley's book open in front of her, and thinking it was time to change the subject. 'There's a bit in here about the foxes. It says that the fox is the messenger of Inari, the rice god. The bib's to keep its fur clean when people offer it fried bean curd, to gain the god's favour.'

'Ours will have to make do with baked beans,' Daniel laughed.

Kit had intended to take pencil and paper to the shrine next day, and try to make a copy of the intricate, carved characters. But that night in bed, she had a better idea. One summer Peter had taken her and Juliet to a church, where you could make brass-rubbings. Using a sheet of thin paper, and a piece of waxy stuff called heelball, Kit had rubbed a picture of a knight in armour, and Juliet had rubbed one of his lady. But, Kit thought, you would get the same effect with a dark wax crayon. So, the following afternoon, while Daniel was weeding the stepping-stone path, Kit sellotaped a sheet of paper over the Japanese characters on the shrine wall, and rubbed a crayon over the lettering underneath. The writing came out quite clearly in white against the black wax, and she was pleased with the result. She wondered whether Kojima would appear again, but there was neither sight nor sense of him in Koraku-en that day.

'I'm going to make a scroll,' she told Daniel, as they walked down the farm road under a white half moon. 'There's a roll of wallpaper in the hall cupboard. I'll copy the characters on to it with a pencil, then ink them in.'

'Mn. That'll be nice,' said Daniel, but vaguely, so that Kit knew he wasn't really paying attention.

'What are you thinking about?' she wanted to know.

'Translation,' said Daniel. 'We aren't going to get any further until we know what these writings mean. D'you suppose that old dame upstairs knows Japanese?'

Kit looked dubious.

'I can't see why she should. Besides, Laura says we're not to speak to her,' she reminded him.

'She sent down the book,' pointed out Daniel, 'so she isn't against what we're doing. And even if she doesn't speak the language, it's possible she knows what the inscriptions mean. I know. Let's write her a note and ask her. She can't object to that.'

Kit wasn't so sure, but she knew by now how determined Daniel could be. There was no point in arguing. So she swallowed her doubts, and when, in the evening, he asked her to sign the note he had written, she added her name without protest.

'Dear Miss Sorley,

We have discovered some Japanese writing in the shrine of Inari, and would very much like to know what it means. Please, can you tell us?

Your sincerely,
Daniel Garth,
Kit Crawford.'

'Dandy-doo,' said Daniel, as he folded the paper and stuffed it into an envelope. 'I'll drop it in her mailbox in the morning, before I go to work.'

They did not have long to wait for a reply. When they came back from the garden the following after-

83

noon, it was on the kitchen table. Written in thin, slightly shaky black writing, it was addressed to Laura.

'Dear Mrs Crawford,
   I have no objection to your children playing in my Japanese garden, but shall be grateful if you will ask them not to involve me in their games. Might I also trouble you to return my book?
Yours sincerely,<br>C. V. Sorley.'

'"Children"!' spluttered Daniel wrathfully. '"Playing"! Of all the ruddy cheek!'

'I told you not to,' said Laura wearily.

'Yes, but all the same,' grumbled Kit, very red in the face. 'What a nasty old creature.'

But Laura shook her head.

'No,' she said. 'You're wrong. It isn't a nasty letter, it's a frightened letter. That old lady's afraid you're going to find out something she doesn't want to know, or that she doesn't want you to know. That's why she's regretting lending you the book, poor little mouse.'

'You always defend her,' muttered Kit.

Laura gave her a pained look.

'I just believe in fairness, Kit,' she said. 'Miss Sorley has done us no harm.'

Kit scowled at the rebuke, but before she could reply Daniel spoke. His indignation seemed suddenly to have cooled.

'Actually, she's cracked,' he said soberly. 'This morning, when I'd dropped the note in the mailbox behind the front door, I thought I might as well go out that way. When I opened the door, she was on the doorstep, coming back from walking her dog. I suppose I startled her, but the way she behaved was loopy. She took one look at me, said, "Oh, my God," and bolted up the stairs as if she had seen a ghost.'

# 13

# 'Clever
Daniel'

'I've had an idea. Let's advertise,' said Daniel, later that evening.

He was sitting by the stove in the kitchen, having a last look through Hester Sorley's book, which Laura said must be returned first thing in the morning. Kit glanced up from the table, where she was painstakingly copying Japanese letters from her rubbing on to a length of flowery cream and pale yellow wallpaper.

'How d'you mean, advertise?' she asked.

'For a translator,' Daniel explained, closing the book. 'We'll put an advertisement in the newspaper, asking anyone who speaks Japanese and wants a job to contact us. We'll have to pay, of course.'

Kit, who had no ready money except the contents of her piggy bank, didn't look keen, but Daniel went on casually, 'It's OK. I'll pay. I saved most of what I earned in Aberdeen, and now Laura's keeping me for next to nothing, so I've got loads of cash. No sweat.'

Kit watched him finding a copy of the *Dundee Courier* to check the advertising rates, then writing the advertisement and a cheque to pay for it. It was at times like this that she was most aware of the gap in their ages; the Daniel who did childish things like playing tiddlywinks and cutting holes in a slice of toast to make funny spectacles could suddenly become a near grown-up, discussing painting, writing cheques. Kit wondered if she would be the same at sixteen, and hoped not. She had always imagined that when she met her real mother she would be cool and very mature.

Returning to the present, however, she said, 'Daniel, listen. Suppose Miss Sorley sees the advertisement. She won't like it, will she?'

'Tough on her,' retorted Daniel, but then, catching Laura's eye, said quickly, 'Look, I've asked for a box number. She won't know it's us, and anyway – what else can we do?'

Since he got no reply to this question, he put on his jacket, took a flashlight and went off to post the letter at the end of the farm road. Kit took up her pencil and went on with her work.

'That's going to look beautiful.' Laura, who was sitting on the other side of the table, giving the foxes a coat of fungicide, leaned over to see how Kit was getting on. 'Isn't it lucky the wallpaper has that pale pattern of chrysanthemums on it? It looks quite Japanese.'

'That's what I thought,' agreed Kit. 'I wonder which room it was used for? I've never seen it anywhere.'

Laura said it certainly wasn't the usual Maddimoss House style.

'How are you going to fill the letters in?' she asked.

'I thought, with a black felt pen,' Kit said.

'In Japan, they do it with a brush,' Laura told her. 'I'm sure I brought a box of painting materials here with me, goodness knows why. I'll look it out for you, if you like.'

'Yes, please. That would be great,' responded Kit.

She heard herself speaking far more warmly than she usually did to Laura, but for once didn't let it worry her.

The rest of the week raced by. Next morning, Laura left Miss Sorley's book on the table at the bottom of the main staircase, from where it was collected by Mrs Brown when she arrived at half-past eight. On Friday, Daniel discovered another set of characters carved on a side wall of the shrine.

親のない子は
入り日をおがむよ
親は入り日の
まんなかによ

Kit made a rubbing of them, and began another scroll. On Saturday the advertisement appeared in the newspaper. *Wanted: Translator of Japanese. Small job. Fee by arrangement.* After that, nothing important happened until the following Wednesday, when a single reply was forwarded from Dundee.

'Where's Netherhill?' asked Daniel, who was reading the letter when Kit arrived home from school.

'It's the village after Tillyrie, going towards Perth,' Kit informed him. 'About ten miles from here. Why?'

Daniel shook his head incredulously.

'It sure is a small world,' he said. 'This is from a guy who lives there. His name's Simon Heale. Says he can do the translation for us, no problem. Go on, then. Say it.'

'Say what?'

'Clever Daniel.'

'That'll be the day,' said Kit witheringly.

But secretly she did think he had been clever. And she had the exhilarating feeling that they were getting somewhere at last.

Daniel wrote a note to Simon Heale, while Kit carefully copied the three Japanese inscriptions on to sheets of writing paper.

'I've told him to 'phone when the translations are ready,' said Daniel, when they had finished. 'We'll go along in the bus and fetch them, then I can pay him at the same time.'

'I just hope he'll be quick. I don't feel I can wait very long,' Kit replied.

Night was falling as they walked down to the post box at the end of the farm road. On the way back, they saw something which Kit, at least, found interesting.

As they approached Maddimoss House, a taxi overtook them, turned in at the main gate, and crunched to a halt on the sweep of gravel outside the front door. Immediately the door opened, and in a shaft of light from the hall Miss Sorley came down the steps. She was wearing her grey overcoat and a black hat, pulled down so that it shaded her face. Following behind was her housekeeper, Mrs Brown, twice her size and carrying a suitcase which she handed to the taxi driver. Then, rather to Kit's surprise, the two women hugged each other, and Miss Sorley got into the back seat. When the taxi passed Kit and Daniel at the gate, she was looking rather pointedly out of the window on the other side.

'I wonder where she's going?' said Kit inquisitively, as she watched the tail-lights weaving down the hill.

It hadn't occurred to her that Miss Sorley would ever leave Maddimoss.

Daniel snorted sourly.

'Thanks for the cheery wave, Miss Sorley, madam,' he bellowed after the departing car.

# 14

# A Weather
# Change

Later on, Kit would remember the night when Miss
Sorley went away as a turning point. Before that,
she had been enjoying a brief spell when her life was
full of comradeship and excitement and mystery.
After that, things began to go badly wrong. It had
nothing to do with Miss Sorley, except that her
departure marked the end of fair weather and the
beginning of storm.

March came in that year not like a lion, or like a
lamb, but stealthily, like a little cat. During the
night thin, unexpected rain began to fall, thickening
by dawn into a white mist which blotted out hills
and river, and folded Maddimoss in a thick mantle.
After two blind, eerie days, the mist gave way to a
downpour that went on, and on, and on, filling
ditches and turning the farm tracks into rivers of
rusty mud. The weeks of enchanted, springlike
weather, which had forced the daffodils and allowed
Kit and Daniel to work every day in the garden,
were over. Which was sad, but sadder still was that
Daniel, who had been so merry and friendly and
pleased with Maddimoss, changed with the weather.

Even before the rain came, there had been signs
of trouble to come. At Laura's suggestion, Daniel

had gone to Edinburgh, to look in the records of Register House for mention of people called Maddimoss. Like all his other investigations, this one had proved fruitless, and he came back late one night, looking dejected. The next day, he had been rattled by a letter from his father, enclosing a brochure entitled *Careers in Medicine*.

'Not fair,' he growled, angrily tearing the brochure in two. 'We agreed we wouldn't talk about it again till Easter.'

Then the rain came.

For the first day or two, Daniel was reasonably pleasant, but as the bad weather continued, he became first restless, then bad-tempered. He began to complain about his job at Whitewells, spent hours slumped in front of the television, and snapped at Kit when she tried to show him her now completed scrolls. This angered Laura, who told him sharply to lay off Kit, and for a heart-stopping moment Kit thought he was going to fetch his things and bang out of the house for ever. But after some mutual glaring between him and Laura, Daniel backed down, to Kit's deep relief.

'Sorry, Puss,' he said, pretending to bang a nail into the top of Kit's head. This was the nearest he ever got to a gesture of affection, and because she thought it was brotherly, Kit loved it. 'The scrolls are ace, honestly. And sorry, Laura,' he added contritely. 'It's this damned weather. I've only got four weeks left to work in the Japanese garden, and there's so much to do.'

And so many mysteries still to solve, thought Kit anxiously. Yet sadly, as the wet, dreary days passed, it mattered less to her what the letters YANAGI meant, or who put the flowers on Kojima's grave. Worry over Daniel and his doings pushed all other concerns into the corners of her mind.

The next thing that happened was that Daniel started going out in the evenings, and staying out until very late. Kit was wakened after midnight by a car's headlights shining through her thin curtains, and heard the sound of voices and banging doors.

'Where do you think he goes?' she asked Laura, after Daniel had declined to answer this question.

Laura looked at her with troubled blue eyes.

'I gather there's a youth club in Tillyrie,' she said, 'although I can't believe it's open till midnight.' She pushed her fair hair back from her face, sighed, and went on, 'I don't like it, Kit, but it's difficult for me to interfere. Daniel's living the way he is with his parents' approval, and they must know the risk they're taking. What he does outside this house really isn't my business.'

'I expect he's made new friends, and goes home with them,' said Kit, trying to choke back the anger and jealousy which this thought aroused in her.

Laura took her hand, and gave it a sympathetic squeeze.

'Never mind, love,' she said. 'I expect it will all come right again when the weather improves.'

But still the rain plashed down, and next afternoon Kit heard rumblings of trouble in another quarter. When she clambered, dripping, on to the bus at Tillyrie post office, Mrs Maxwell was already on board, coming home from Perth market. When Kit saw her pink face protruding from a hole in her green waterproof cape, she waved, and went to sit beside her. For a few moments they talked about the weather, then Kit remembered something.

'Mrs Maxwell,' she said, 'do you know that Miss Sorley has gone away?'

She was still curious to know where Miss Sorley had gone, and reckoned, rightly, that if anyone could enlighten her it would be Mrs Maxwell. The farmer's wife nodded, with the faint air of disapproval which she always assumed when Miss Sorley was mentioned.

'To London, so I hear from Ismay Brown. The lady has business to attend to. Ismay's worried she'll be knocked down in the street – says she's as blind as a bat. But not too blind to read her bank statement, I dare say.'

Kit laughed, then felt disloyal. Why she should, when she didn't even know Miss Sorley, she wasn't sure; perhaps she was just ashamed of laughing at such a hard-hearted remark. But before she could blame Mrs Maxwell, she had herself been unkind about Miss Sorley.

'Daniel says she's loopy,' she remarked, and wished too late that she hadn't.

But Mrs Maxwell had lost interest in Miss Sorley. It was Daniel's name which made her swell indignantly, and the corners of her mouth tightened with displeasure. It went through Kit's mind that Mrs Maxwell was in a terrible mood today, and she wished she had sat somewhere else. But she couldn't avoid hearing what Mrs Maxwell had to say.

'Maybe she is,' she snapped, 'but that Daniel has troubles of his own. He's late every morning, his work's a disgrace, and Dad says he can smell drink on him. Well, the last bit's no business of mine, but the rest is, and you can tell him from me, we won't stand for much more of it. Him and his earring!'

Kit felt her cheeks go hot, which was strange, because the rest of her was like ice. She wanted to be angry, and defend Daniel, but no words came. It was true that nowadays he was always still in the kitchen when she left for school at ten past eight.

'Cool it, Puss,' he had said that very morning, when she had begged him to hurry up. 'Old Maxwell hasn't even got a watch.'

She also knew that it was probably true that Daniel's work was poor; she had watched him getting bored with the job. As for the charge that Daniel was smelling of drink, she wanted to shout that it couldn't possibly be true. But how could she, when she knew that Daniel had been expelled for getting drunk at school, and he wouldn't tell Laura where he went in the evenings?

A black hood of depression descended on Kit as she got off the bus and walked up the hill beside Mrs Maxwell, into a wall of rain. Daniel was in danger, and all the grown-ups could say was, 'It's no business of mine.' Shouldn't Mr Maxwell, or Laura, talk to Daniel, and give him some friendly advice? Should she, as Mrs Maxwell seemed to think? But if she did – and it always came back to this in the end – might he not lose his temper, and storm out? She might never see him, or hear from him again.

Of course, Kit knew that in a month's time Daniel would have to go home, but so far she had made the knowledge tolerable by imagining letters and 'phone calls, and hoping that in the summer Daniel's parents would invite her to stay. What she couldn't contemplate was the desolation she'd feel if he left in anger, and for good. How could she bear a life with no Daniel, tormented anew by dreams of Juliet? Yet the feeling that she was not acting a true friend's part bore down on her like a heavy weight.

As she took off her wet coat and hung it up behind the kitchen door, Kit decided on what she knew was a coward's way out. She would wait a few days and hope that, by some miracle, Daniel would sort out his problems without her. If not, she would try to pluck up courage to tackle him later on.

But sadly, it was already too late for anyone to prevent the events which were about to unfold.

# 15

# Trouble at
# Tillyrie

That evening, the rain stopped at last. The clouds rolled back, and for the first time in a fortnight the sky showed a scatter of trembling stars. Then overnight a strong, drying wind sprang up, so that by morning the stuccoed front of Maddimoss House was patched wet and dry, and the earthy torrent rushing down the farm road had been reduced to trickles. In the afternoon, Daniel told Kit that he had been to the Japanese garden, and reckoned that if the rain held off, by the next day it would be dry enough to get back to work.

'I think we should concentrate on the area around the shrine of Inari,' he told her. 'There's no way I'm going to have time for everything, so we may as well do one bit properly. Do you agree?'

Kit nodded eagerly. She didn't really care what they did, as long as they did it together. The thought that they might see Kojima again no longer perturbed her. Indeed, she thought she would rather like it.

'I agree,' she said.

'Dandy-doo,' said Daniel. 'I'll nip to Tillyrie after lunch tomorrow, and get wood preservative for the shrine. And two brushes, so that you can help me to slap it on.'

This sounded so like old times that Kit was comforted. She thought optimistically that perhaps the danger which had brushed Daniel had now passed by. But it was not to be.

Kit had hoped that Daniel would stay at home that night. Their normal little conversation in the afternoon had made her long more than ever to have the friendly, pleasant evenings they used to have restored. So she was disappointed when Daniel rose from the table at ten to seven, and went off hurriedly to his room to get changed. Kit was helping Laura to wash up when he passed through the kitchen, on his way to catch the last bus to Tillyrie at twenty past.

'I thought he might have stayed in tonight,' Kit said wistfully to Laura, who sighed as she replied.

'Not much chance of that, my love. He's got the habit of going out now, I'm afraid.'

Kit collected the clean cutlery and took it to the dresser, trying not to wonder what Daniel was doing in Tillyrie. For once, she was glad she had a lot of homework. She badly needed something to concentrate her mind.

When the kitchen was tidy, Kit went off to her room, and Laura sat down at the table to get on with painting the foxes. She had coated them with chestnut wood preservative, and given their bibs eight coats of red gloss to resemble lacquer. Now she was gilding their paws with a small brush, and a steady, patient hand. When Kit had done her maths, written a story and revised history for a test next day, she had a shower and put on her pyjamas and dressing-gown. It was twenty past nine when she came back into the kitchen, and simultaneously a key was turned slowly in the lock on the outside door. Kit and Laura looked at each other with startled eyes.

'Daniel?' said Kit.

She hadn't expected to see him again until morning.

Daniel came in and locked the door behind him. He had his hood up, and pulled forward over his face, like a monk's. He didn't speak, and Kit watched in astonishment as he slouched across the floor with his head ducked, and one hand raised furtively in front of his face. He would have gone out without a word, but before he could open the hall door Laura had risen from the table and placed herself in front of him.

'No, you don't,' she said quietly.

Kit heard Daniel swear, and for a tense, nasty moment she thought he was going to push Laura aside. But then suddenly he seemed to crumple. Laura leaned forward and gently twitched the hood back from his face.

'My dear boy,' she said, horrified. 'What have you done?'

Daniel's face was a sorry sight. His left eye was the colour of port wine, and almost closed. He had a cut lip, and a mixture of dried and fresh blood around his nose. On his jaw was a bruise obviously imprinted by somebody's knuckles. Kit burst into tears.

But Laura went into action. Taking Daniel by the shoulders, she steered him to a chair and pushed him into it. She unzipped his bloodstained jacket, and told him to slip it off. Then she fetched a bowl of cold water and the first aid box from the dresser drawer.

'Stop bawling, Kit, and make Daniel some tea,' she ordered, as she soaked a pad of cotton wool and held it against Daniel's eye.

It was a long time since Kit had been spoken to so crisply, and the shock steadied her. She filled the kettle, and put a tea-bag into a mug. Then she watched nervously as Laura worked on Daniel's injuries. He winced and hissed a bit, but nobody spoke until she had finished, and Daniel was seated beside the stove with his fingers wrapped around a mug of hot tea. Then Laura said, 'I can't force you, but I think you should tell me who did this. If there were witnesses, I can call the police.'

An expression of panic appeared in Daniel's open eye.

'For God's sake, don't do that,' he begged. 'You see, I started it.'

Kit, who had settled on a chair at the stove end of the table, gasped in dismay.

'You mean, you hit somebody first?' she asked.

'Yes.' Daniel glanced at her, then turned away from the reproachful look on her face. 'I'll tell you what happened,' he said to Laura, 'but please, promise you won't call the police. If my dad found out about this –'

He looked as if he was going to cry.

'All right,' agreed Laura. 'But tell me anyway.'

Daniel was silent for a moment, then it all began to come out.

'When I started at Whitewells,' he said, 'there

was another lad there, older than me, called Greg. He got the boot at the end of my first week for nicking Mrs M's egg money, but we'd had a few laughs, and I met him again one day when I was in Tillyrie, at the bank. I've been meeting him and his mates, and some girls who hang around with them, having a few drinks –' He stopped abruptly, appalled by his own indiscretion. 'Er, that is,' he mumbled.

'Daniel,' said Laura gravely, 'have you been drinking in the hotel at Tillyrie? It's against the law, and the manager could be in big trouble for serving you.'

But Daniel shook his head.

'There's no way I could pass for eighteen,' he said. 'Greg went in and got the beer, and we took it up to an old cabin in Frankly Wood. But tonight there was a disco at Tillyrie Youth Club –'

'And?'

'There's this guy Stringer,' said Daniel, fingering his jaw. 'He's a biker. Comes out from Dundee, looking for trouble. He's never liked me, and tonight he wouldn't leave me alone. He kept bugging me about my English accent, and what he calls my posh boy's clothes. Greg and the girls laughed. They think Stringer's great, but they're scared of him too.'

'So you hit Stringer,' breathed Kit, admiration overcoming her disapproval.

'No. I hit Greg,' corrected Daniel ruefully. 'His stupid face got in my way. Then Stringer hit me. There was a hell of a punch-up, and we were all thrown out on the pavement. I think I'd have been killed if Mr Maxwell's dairyman hadn't been one of the guys running the show. He came out and saw the rest off, then he brought me home. Laura –'

'What?'

'Are you going to kick me out?'

Laura looked at him thoughtfully, then she said, 'If I did, would you go straight home?'

'To Birmingham?'

'Sure. How many homes have you got?'

Daniel grinned faintly.

'No,' he said. 'Not yet.'

'Then until you have that home to go back to after you've made a fool of yourself, you may as well have this one,' Laura replied. 'Besides —' for the first time she smiled at Daniel '— if I kicked you out, Kit would never speak to me again.'

At this point, a very odd sensation came over Kit. She wanted to run to Laura and give her a hug. She didn't, of course. But it was certainly what, for a moment, she wanted to do.

# 16

# The Shrine
## of Inari

It would seem strange, afterwards, that no one had even wondered whether the events at Tillyrie Youth Club might have an aftermath. Perhaps they were all too eager to put a dreadful night behind them, and forget it. And to be fair, it would have been very difficult to foresee, let alone take precautions against what actually happened.

It was obvious, the morning after, that Daniel wasn't fit for work, and Laura made him stay in bed. While Kit was eating her breakfast, she 'phoned Whitewells, only to find that the Maxwells already knew what had occurred. Adam Gifford, the dairyman and youth club leader, had looked in at the farm on his way home from Tillyrie. Kit, sitting near the telephone, could hear the conversation clearly, and was surprised, after Mrs Maxwell's remarks on the bus, to hear her sounding so sympathetic.

'Adam says the louts had been picking on Daniel all evening,' she told Laura indignantly, 'and what happened was far more their fault than his. Adam's warned them off, and Dad will go by Greg Wilson's place today, and have a word with his father. All the same, it would be sensible if Daniel kept away from Tillyrie in the evenings, from now on.'

Laura said she was sure Daniel would agree, and was about to ring off when Mrs Maxwell added, 'Oh, by the way, Mrs Crawford. Will you ask Kit please to forgive me for being so ill-natured the day we travelled together on the bus? Tell her my bunions were killing me.'

Kit giggled, but she knew that Mrs Maxwell was much troubled by her bunions, and gladly forgave her.

The next few days passed peacefully. Daniel's face got worse, then quickly better, and by the weekend he was fit for work again. He showed no inclination to leave Maddimoss, and Kit had a happy time helping him to brush wood preservative on to the shrine of Inari. Koraku-en was beginning to look good. The grass was trimmed and the gravel raked in a wavy pattern around the stone lantern. The moss was emerald after the rain, buds were swelling, and white wood anemones were opening under the rhododendrons. Kojima didn't show himself, but sometimes Kit felt that he was near. The weather was clear and calm once more, and she had a wonderful, relieved feeling that the bad days had been a nightmare interlude, now over. In fact, a storm of a different kind was still to come.

Kit's bedroom faced east, towards the city of Dundee, ten miles away. The city itself was invisible from her window, blocked by the conifers of Sparrowlea Wood, but Kit was used to seeing its great red aura staining the night sky. That was why, when she switched off the bathroom light on Monday evening, she wasn't at once alerted by what she saw through the uncurtained upper sash of the window.

She was back in her room when it struck her that something was wrong. The bathroom window faced west. There shouldn't have been a red light in the sky.

With her heart beginning to thud violently, Kit ran in her pyjamas back through the hall to the bathroom. The light she had seen was brighter now, a tall column flickering rosily above the dark wood. There was a fire, in the Japanese garden.

Laura had had a letter from Peter that morning, and had gone to bed early with a headache. It didn't even occur to Kit to rouse her. Instead, she fled silently across the hall to Daniel's room, and threw open the door. He was in bed in the dark, though not asleep. In the beam of light from the hall, Kit saw him start up in alarm from under his duvet.

'Hang on, Puss —'

'Oh, Daniel,' sobbed Kit. 'Please come. There's a fire in the Japanese garden. You can see it from the bathroom window —'

Daniel leapt out of bed, and shot past her. It took him seconds to reach the bathroom, and confirm what she had said.

'Quick! Get dressed,' he urged her. 'It isn't big. If we hurry, we can put it out with water from the lake before it spreads.'

Kit didn't even pause to think what a crazy idea this was. Frantically she dragged on trousers, a jersey and her boots, and chased the thin ray from Daniel's flashlight up the dark farm road. As she pounded along the path through the wood, she could see a pink arch at the end of the tunnel. Beyond it was the torii, sharp and black against a deeper, sinister light.

Daniel's despairing cry, 'It's the shrine, Puss,' confirmed her fear, then they were leaping along the stepping-stone path towards a fire-bright Koraku-en.

The shrine of Inari was burning like a huge torch. Gold and amber flames burst from its roof, illuminating the dark wood all around. In front of the steps, the gravel was trampled and the stone lantern toppled, but not until she saw empty paraffin cans thrown down on the grass did Kit understand, with a pang of terror, what had caused this catastrophe. She heard Daniel say chokily, 'We can't tackle this. We must get –' Help was the word, but it was too late. Suddenly dark figures rose out of the undergrowth, and moved cat-like towards them. In the nightmarish light, Kit saw that they had their hoods up, and scarves tied over their faces.

'Got them,' said a gloating voice.

'I told you they'd come,' sniggered another.

Kit and Daniel had walked into a trap.

For one mad moment, Kit thought she could get away. She saw two figures leap on Daniel, but in front of her there seemed to be an opening among the trees, to the left of the shrine. She ran towards it, but a figure rose in front of her, and tripped her up. As she fell, another came, and she realized with shock that her attackers were girls. One put a bony knee hard into her back, crushing her chest against the ground, and pushed her head down brutally into the needly moss. The other sat heavily on her legs to stop her kicking. Kit felt a terrible pain in her chest, and she couldn't breathe. But, just as she thought she was being murdered, a tiny, calm cell in her brain told her that she still had an arm free. It also reminded her where she was. Pushing out her left arm and groping with her hand, she found what she knew must be there. Her fingers closed around the end of a rope, and with her last scrap of strength, she pulled.

At once the sweet, sickening note of the bronze bell rang out, shattering and vibrating and filling the garden with its dreadful sound. Kit felt her attackers loosen their hold, and as she rolled away saw them bent double, with their arms over their heads, whimpering and not knowing what to do.

Then Kojima came. As Daniel somersaulted across the scorching grass to Kit's side, a great wind blew through the garden, bending the treetops, ruffling the lake and gusting in the bushes around the burning shrine. Huddling against Daniel, Kit saw the ghostly gardener emerge from the flames. Small and gentle before, he now seemed swollen by fury to the size of a sumō wrestler. His eyes glared menacingly in a purple, fiery face, while the flames behind him flickered eerily through his vast, semi-transparent body. Kit was terrified, even though she knew he was on her side.

As for the vandals, they were driven almost mad with fear. As Kojima advanced on them with his right forearm vengefully raised, they staggered to their feet and fled, howling and crashing like wild animals through the undergrowth towards the lake. Daniel told Kit afterwards that Kojima had dwindled to his normal size, smiled and bowed to them before he melted away among the pines. But Kit had no recollection of that. For her, suddenly the light went out.

# 17

# Working Things
# Out

When Kit woke up, she was lying on Laura's bed. She knew where she was because she could see, fuzzily, the portraits of herself and Juliet on the wall opposite. Laura was gently wiping dirt from her face with a damp sponge. Kit felt as if there were a tight iron band round her chest, and when she breathed in a knife seemed to stab between her ribs.

'Laura, I can't breathe,' she sobbed.

'Yes, you can,' said Laura calmly. 'Take little breaths, and don't panic. The doctor's coming. Lie still.'

Kit closed her eyes, and into the darkness came memory, of the fire, and the attack, and the ghost.

'Where's Daniel?' she asked hoarsely.

'He's all right,' said Laura, in the same even, reassuring tone. 'Mrs Maxwell is looking after him, and Mr Maxwell and his men have put out the fire.'

'Did they catch – those people?'

'No. Something must have scared them off. When I woke and realized you'd gone, I rang Mr Maxwell, but by the time we reached the garden, the vandals were screaming up the lake side as if they'd seen a ghost. Now stop worrying. I think I hear the doctor's car.'

Kit was hazy about what happened after that. She knew that Dr Hay was looking in her eyes with a small flashlight, and winced as his cool fingers probed her ribs. Vaguely she heard, 'Nothing broken,' and, 'Sore for a day or two.' Then he was gone, and Laura was undressing her and helping her under the duvet. There were pills to swallow, then she fell asleep.

Always, afterwards, Kit remembered the next two days as among the most important in her life, because it was then she discovered what it was like to be Juliet. All the things she had envied her sister now came to her. Lying in Laura's bed, she opened get-well cards from Granny and Miss Whitaker, and admired a bunch of pink tulips which Daniel had gone to Perth to buy. Mrs Maxwell came to visit her, bringing cream and eggs, and Miss Sorley's housekeeper, Mrs Brown, handed in a puzzle book and a bag of toffees. Laura read stories, played games and cooked Kit's favourite dishes.

At the same time, Kit learned that there was a price to be paid for these treats. Her bruised chest hurt badly. Sometimes she felt tired and cross, and wished everyone would go away and leave her alone. That was when she found herself looking at the portrait of Juliet which Laura had painted years ago, and understanding for the first time what it had felt like to spend the night in a painful struggle for breath, and how exhausted Juliet had felt in the morning. Kit was an honest girl, and as she looked into the blank, painted blue eyes she didn't pretend that she felt, or would ever feel, affection for Juliet.

But with understanding, both her hatred and her guilt faded; Juliet took her place in the past, and stopped being the most important person in Kit's life.

On the second day, Laura allowed Daniel to visit Kit. After lunch he came with the tulips, and paper and pencils to play noughts and crosses. He sat down on the bed and made a face at Kit.

'Jeeze!' he said. 'Your mum's a terror. She's worse than my dad.'

'How come?' inquired Kit, surprised.

Daniel rolled his eyes.

'She gave me one hell of a row for taking you to the garden the night of the fire,' he said. 'Called me a stupid fool with a teaspoonful of brain, and said if any real harm had come to you she'd have killed me with her bare hands.'

'Some lady,' said Kit, repressing a gratified smirk.

'It's true, though,' said Daniel, looking contrite. 'Apologies, Puss.'

'Forget it,' said Kit. 'You couldn't have stopped me. Hey, Daniel – Kojima was awesome, wasn't he?'

Daniel nodded.

'I suppose he was furious,' he said, 'because it was his special place.'

'Mn,' said Kit thoughtfully. 'There is that, of course. But I think he wanted to save us, because we're his friends.' The old question, 'Why us?' rose in her mind again, but she didn't ask it, because she knew Daniel didn't have an answer. 'Is the shrine gone for good?' she asked.

The pain in Daniel's grey eyes made her look away.

'Yes,' he growled savagely, 'and the police won't do anything, since I can't positively identify the stinkers who did it – though I know they were Stringer and Greg and their girlfriends. I'm the big-mouth who told them about the garden, for God's sake. So they've got away with it, damn them all.'

Kit grinned wickedly.

'Oh, I don't know,' she said airily. 'They saw a ghost, didn't they? I bet they're scared out of their pin-head minds. Think about it.'

Daniel thought, and cheered up considerably.

'Mr Maxwell and Adam are going to clear the site before Miss Sorley gets back,' he told Kit. 'Mr M thinks she'll be upset when she finds out what's happened, though I don't see why. Surely if she'd cared about the garden, she'd have looked after it properly.'

Kit shook her head. Whatever the mystery at Maddimoss, it always seemed to involve Miss Sorley.

'At least we got the foxes out,' she said, 'and the Japanese inscriptions. She can have those.'

Daniel nodded, but Kit knew his mind had turned to something else.

'Mrs M says I should tell you this. She thinks you're worrying about me,' he blurted out. 'I've had a long talk with both the Maxwells. They were thinking of giving me the sack for being late and not pulling my weight, but they're going to give me another chance.' He grinned sheepishly and added, 'I've had to promise to go easy on the booze, and stop hanging around with thugs and vandals.'

A vast wave of relief, happiness and gratitude to the Maxwells swept over Kit, but she knew Daniel would be embarrassed if she let her feelings show.

'Great. Let's play noughts and crosses,' was all she said.

The next night, when Kit was feeling much better, Laura came to bed early. She climbed in beside Kit, made herself comfortable and said, 'Do you feel like a talk?'

'What about?' asked Kit.

'Us.'

'Oh. Sure,' said Kit, wondering what on earth was coming next.

Laura took a moment to put her thoughts in order, then she said, 'Kit, you do know, don't you, that it's very unlikely Peter will come back to us?'

Kit had known this for a long time, but hearing it put into words was a shock, all the same. It was as if once spoken, it must be true, and certain consequences must follow.

'Has he said so?' she asked.

'Not exactly,' Laura replied, 'but I had a letter the other day. It was all about a girl he's working with called Rosemary Gill. He's been surfing and going to barbecues with her, and next weekend he's flying up to Queensland to stay with her family. I reckoned he was trying to tell me something.'

'He's a rotten pig,' burst out Kit, surprising herself.

She had always thought she preferred Peter to Laura. But Laura shook her head.

'No. To be fair, he isn't,' she said. 'This is all my fault.'

Kit went on surprising herself.

'It is not,' she cried indignantly. 'It's his fault. He started all the quarrels, the mean slob.'

This was true, although she had only just realized it.

'Well, maybe,' said Laura. 'But I should have reacted differently. I should have remembered how terribly unhappy he was.'

'You were unhappy too,' Kit insisted stubbornly.

Laura gave her a grateful glance.

'Yes, but it was more complicated for Peter,' she said. 'You see, he really idolized Juliet. Afterwards he couldn't understand why he had lost his favourite child, but I still had mine.'

Kit felt as if the world was turning upside down.

'What? You mean, I was your favourite?' she stuttered. 'But I thought – that is, I'd never have guessed.'

'Well, no. I hope not,' replied Laura. 'Parents aren't supposed to show favouritism, and I used to get narked with Peter because I thought he did. I remember once hearing him telling you to be sporting, and let Juliet win at Snakes and Ladders. Did you ever hear anything so absurd? But there's a difference between loving and liking. Of course I loved Juliet. She was my child. But she didn't have an affectionate nature, and because she was ill, and we gave in to her so much, she was spoiled and grumpy and demanding as well. Whereas you were such a cosy little creature. I've always loved dark, brown-eyed kids, and I adored you from the very first day I saw you.' She sighed, and went on, 'While Juliet was alive, Peter accepted that we loved you both, but each had a private preference. But after she died, I'm afraid it was a different story. He remembered every critical remark I'd ever made about Juliet, and how I'd said that since her asthma was improving, it was time she learned she wasn't the centre of the world. But she was the centre of Peter's world, and he'll never forgive me. As things have turned out, I can't forgive myself.'

Kit felt as if a great lump of ice was melting inside her. She heard Laura choking back tears, and wanted to comfort her as she'd never wanted anything before.

'Look, you don't have to feel bad,' she said earnestly. 'You were always kind and loving to Juliet. She couldn't have known you were sometimes cross with her, because you never showed it.' And because suddenly it was easy to be generous, she added, 'If Juliet could only have a short life, I'm glad you made it a happy one.'

It was a lie, really, but as she spoke the words, somehow they became true. Laura squeezed her hand.

'At least you have nothing to regret,' she said. 'I used to be amazed by your patience with Juliet. She was so bossy and demanding, but you never snapped back at her. I think a lot of you for that.'

Then Kit had a terrible urge to let everything come tumbling out, how Laura was mistaken, how she'd hated Juliet, and believed herself unloved. But she managed not to. It seemed both she and Laura had been wrong about everything, but whereas Laura's story had brought comfort to her, hers would hurt Laura dreadfully. That was the last thing Kit wanted now.

So she closed her lips over the past, and presently Laura said, 'Anyway, the question is – what do you and I do now? I suppose I have rights to half of what Peter and I own jointly, and there must be some way of getting our money out of that quagmire with half a house on it. Maybe I can find a job. We'll manage, won't we?'

'Yes,' said Kit. 'Only –'

'Only what?'

'I'd quite like to stay around here, if it's possible.'

She didn't mean in Maddimoss House. She meant near the Maxwells, and the Japanese garden, and Daniel, who was determined to come back as soon as he could. She would have been surprised by Laura's reply if she'd had any capacity for surprise left.

'Yes, I'm coming to like it too.' Laura gave Kit a half smile, then went on resolutely, 'However, first things first. On Saturday, you and I are going to have a day out.'

'We are?'

'Yes. We'll go to Dundee, and in the morning I'll have my hair cut. Then we'll have a nice lunch, and treat ourselves to some new clothes. You must be sick of being the only kid at Tillyrie School with a witch for a mother.'

It was a brave speech. Squealing a denial, Kit rolled over, put her arms round Laura, and gave her a hug. Then she gave her several more, as if she were making up for lost time.

'Laura, I was wondering,' she said later, when the light was out. 'Do you want Peter to come back?'

Laura answered without hesitation.

'No. After all that's happened, I think it will be better for us all to have a new start. His coming back now would cause more problems than it would solve.'

'That's what I think,' Kit agreed.

# 18

# Yanagi C.S.

During the next week, Daniel and Kit did what they could to restore the desecrated Koraku-en. Only a blackened square now marked the place where the shrine of Inari had stood, but with Mr Maxwell's help Daniel righted the stone lantern, while Kit raked the gravel. Daniel dug out some blackened shrubs, and tidied up the singed grass.

'The rest will grow again,' he said, 'given time.'

On Friday, when Kit got home from school, Daniel was impatiently waiting with news.

'Simon Heale rang up,' he told her excitedly. 'He's got our translations ready, so don't take your coat off. There's a bus to Netherhill at ten past four.'

'Great,' said Kit. 'Is it OK, Laura?'

Laura, who was sitting at the table giving the foxes a last, careful coat of varnish, nodded agreeably. With her fair hair neatly cut and a striped smock over her new dove-coloured pinafore dress she looked years younger, and almost as beautiful as Kit remembered her long ago.

'Of course,' she said. 'I'd take you in the car, only I think I'd better stay here. Miss Sorley's coming home this evening, and Mrs Brown has asked me to break the news to her about the shrine being destroyed.'

'Why can't Mrs Brown tell her?' inquired Kit curiously.

Laura shook her head.

'Don't ask me,' she said. 'She just says she can't bear to see Miss Sorley hurt. I hadn't realized how close they are. I didn't know how to say no, so I said yes. Can't say I'm looking forward to it, though.'

This was the old Laura, Kit thought, the one who couldn't say no to anyone.

It was a lovely bus run along the foot of the Braes, at the end of a perfect spring day. As afternoon dipped gently towards night, low mist was unravelling like wool across the Carse, but the sky was still blue, and the trees faintly green with the suggestion of coming leaf. When the bus stopped by the wall of Frankly churchyard, Kit could look down from the window at Kojima's grave. In the black vase were two white narcissi and a dried flower head.

Simon Heale's house was the last in Netherhill, a red sandstone cottage sunk behind a wall, so that only the slate roof and chimneys were visible from the road. There were four steps down from the gate, and Kit was fascinated to see, outside the front door, a stone lantern similar to the one in Koraku-en. She was even more fascinated, when Simon Heale opened the door, to see that he was young, and looked Japanese. He smiled and shook hands in an absent-minded way, and took them into a small white-walled room with blue curtains and Japanese vases arranged on top of low bookcases. There was a computer on a small table, and files and papers all over the floor. Behind the clock on the mantelpiece there was a brown envelope, which Simon took down and handed to Daniel.

'I hope it wasn't a lot of trouble,' Kit said politely.

Simon grinned at her.

'Lord, no,' he said. 'My mother's Japanese, and I was brought up in Japan. Where did you find these writings?'

Kit explained about the shrine of Inari, adding sadly that it had recently been burned down by vandals. But Simon's response to this news was vague.

'Oh, yes. I've heard of a Japanese garden at Maddimoss,' he said, 'though I've never got round to looking at it. I'm up to my eyeballs in work at the University, and I never have time for anything else.' He laughed, and added, 'I only answered your advertisement out of curiosity.'

'Do you teach Japanese?' asked Kit.

'No. I'm doing a PhD in Computer Studies,' Simon replied. Kit was dying to ask him whether his mother was related to someone called Kojima, and if he ever took flowers to Frankly churchyard, but since he hadn't asked them to sit down, this didn't seem the right time. When Simon added, 'I'm terribly busy,' Kit recognized a heavy hint.

'You must come and see the garden some time,' she said.

Simon didn't say he would, or would not. Kit felt disappointed as she watched Daniel put the envelope in his pocket, and heard him offer to pay Simon for his work. They were about to be shown out, and there was no reason why they should ever see this young man again. But there was a surprise to come.

Simon refused Daniel's offer, saying that it had

only taken him a few minutes, and was a pleasure. He opened the door, and switched on the light in the previously dark hall. A lamp sprang to life on a polished table, and as Kit and Daniel left Simon's study, two spotlights drew their eyes to an unframed oil painting which almost completely covered one wall. At first it seemed only a profusion of luminous colour, pink, peach, yellow, green and gold. You had to concentrate before it began to take shape as a picture, then you saw trees and grass and deep, still water, shadowed with subtle mauve against an evening sky. High in one corner was a small crimson sun, and across the foreground a pine branch, with blue bursts of needles hanging down.

Daniel, who wanted to be a painter, whistled in admiration, but Kit stared silently. At first she was puzzled, but then recognition came.

In the sitting-room of the Edinburgh house there had been a painting, smaller than this, which was Laura's proudest possession. It too was unframed, but the colours had been the same, and Kit remembered a little red sun, like a child's ball, behind the tasselled branches of a pine. Scarcely able to believe what she knew, she glanced down at the bottom right-hand corner of the huge canvas. Of course, the artist's signature was the same. 'Yanagi C.S.' Yanagi. The word embroidered on the shawl. That was where she had seen it before.

'My mum has a painting like this,' she told Simon, hoping she didn't sound as odd as she felt. 'Not so big, but similar. It's in store, till our new house is ready.'

Simon raised his straight black eyebrows.

'Really?' he said. 'I hope she has it insured. This one belongs to my mother, and apparently it's worth a mint. But of course!' Suddenly he laughed. 'I'd forgotten. You must know the artist.'

'Must I?' asked Kit, mystified.

'Yes. It's Clare Sorley,' Simon replied. 'She lives at Maddimoss, doesn't she? I suppose she's old now, but she's very distinguished. This is one of her early works, from the 1940s. At that time every picture she painted had a tiny red sun in the sky, and a pine tree.'

Kit could scarcely believe her ears. But as she struggled to take in this astounding information, Daniel asked what proved to be a vital question.

'Why would she sign it "Yanagi"?'

Simon shook his dark head.

'I've no idea. I don't think anyone knows much about her,' he said. 'Apparently she's always been a very shy, private person. All I can tell you is that she signs all her paintings like that. It's a Japanese word, meaning "Green Willow". My mother says there's a strong Japanese influence in Sorley's work. Weren't her parents travellers in Japan?'

'They made the Japanese garden,' Daniel said.

# 19

# Secrets of
# the Shrine

'I suppose it's possible,' said Kit dubiously. 'Japanese writing's very different from English, isn't it? Still, it's hard to believe that this really equals all of that.'

As soon as they had arrived home, Daniel had unfurled Kit's scrolls across the kitchen table, and placed the little wooden board from the shrine beside them. The table was covered with lively, flamboyant Japanese characters; in comparison the five short lines of English on the paper which Daniel had taken from Simon's envelope seemed thin and disappointing.

> *I must depart now.*
> *But, like the pine*
> *At the peak of Inaba,*
> *Should I hear you pine for me*
> *I shall return to you.*

'I expected a proper message, not a poem,' admitted Daniel, frowning. 'Simon's written at the bottom that it's by a famous Japanese poet called Ariwara Yukihira, who lived more than a thousand years ago. Why would Kojima spend time carving that on the wall of the shrine? I just hope we haven't jumped to the wrong conclusion.'

'Meaning?'

'That he wasn't really trying to tell us anything after all.'

Kit pursed her lips as she considered this. Then she said, 'I'm sure he was, Daniel. Think of the day we saw him in Koraku-en, the day you found the foxes and the wooden board. He was absolutely delighted. I just wonder –'

'What?'

'Whether he had already tried to tell someone else something, and failed.'

Kit had often been teased by Daniel, but she couldn't complain that he hadn't taken her ideas seriously. Now he sat down by the table, and looked at her with questioning grey eyes.

'You've lost me, Puss,' he admitted. 'But fire away.'

Kit glanced at the poem again, then said pensively, 'It is quite ghostly, if you look at it that way. I think perhaps Kojima was using the words of a poem he knew to say something he couldn't find words of his own for. Didn't it say in Hester Sorley's book that she ticked him off for wasting time carving in 1930?'

'Yes,' agreed Daniel.

'Well, then. That was the year he died,' pointed out Kit. 'Suppose that when he wrote, "I must depart now," he knew that he was dying, and "If I hear you pine for me, I shall return to you" was a message for someone he loved, and didn't want to leave? After all, we know he did return.'

Daniel gave her a look of admiration which made her blush.

'Puss, that's brilliant,' he said sincerely. 'And if he didn't get his message through then, that would explain why he's got in touch with us now. He wants us to help him deliver it. Only –' Daniel paused, wrinkling his forehead '– who on earth can he still want to contact after all this time?'

This would have been a perfect moment for Kit to air her theory that Simon Heale's Japanese mother must be the link with Kojima, the arranger of flowers on his grave. But before she could open her mouth, there was an interruption. The kitchen door flew open, and Laura appeared. Her cheeks were flushed, and she was unusually bright-eyed.

'I've been drinking. Two large gins,' she announced defiantly, as she flopped into an armchair beside the stove, and stretched out her emerald green legs on the rug. Ignoring Kit, who was seething with disapproval, she looked straight at Daniel. 'Do you know,' she demanded dramatically, 'who that old woman is? She's Clare Sorley, for heaven's sake, the idol of my youth and probably the greatest British painter of her generation. She's been living over my head for six months, and I never even guessed.'

'We knew that, and you'd better have some black coffee,' said Kit repressively, picking up the kettle.

'The guy we visited this afternoon had one of her paintings,' Daniel explained, grinning widely. 'It was ace, I must say.'

'How did Miss Sorley take the news about the shrine?' inquired Kit, as she spooned a lot of coffee into a mug.

'She knew,' said Laura. 'The taxi-driver told her, coming from the station.'

'Was she upset?'

'I'm sure she was, but she'd had time to get her feelings under control. She thanked me for coming, but she seemed to prefer talking about other things.' Laura took the mug Kit handed to her, and brought it over to the table. 'Did you get the translations?' she asked.

'Only this,' Daniel told her, giving her the poem to read. 'Do you reckon all that Japanese writing could be condensed into five lines of English?'

'No, of course not,' Laura said. 'It's the translation of that scroll.' She pointed with her finger. 'It's the only one with five lines.'

'Not bad, after two large gins,' teased Daniel.

But not much help either, as Kit gloomily pointed out.

'I reckon Simon just forgot to translate the other two,' she said, 'or else lost them in all that litter in his sitting-room. Now we'll have to go through all the rigmarole of contacting him again, and he probably won't answer for yonks. What a bore.'

Even as she was speaking, however, a car's headlights swept over the kitchen window, and they heard the crunch of wheels on the gravel outside the back door. Kit ran to the window and peered out.

'Amazing! It's Simon,' she squealed, hurrying to open the door.

Simon was in a hurry, and full of apologies.

'Sorry, sorry, sorry,' he said, holding out two more sheets of paper to Daniel. 'I found these under the table after you'd gone. Must have forgotten to put them in the envelope. Can't stay, but – hey, wait a minute!' he added, catching sight of the scrolls on the table. 'These are nice. Who made them?'

'Me,' said Kit.

'Great,' enthused Simon, beaming at her. 'You should learn Japanese.'

'Yes, I intend to. I'm going to work in Japan when I'm grown up,' replied Kit, and felt peeved that no one was paying much attention as she announced an important plan she'd only that minute thought of.

Simon had picked up the little wooden board.

'Do you know what this is?' he asked Daniel, who shook his head.

'We found it in the shrine of Inari,' he explained.

'It's called an ema,' Simon told him. 'In Japan people write prayers on boards like this, and hang them up in Shinto shrines to ask help from the kami, or gods. But look – I must go. I've got so much work on hand. We'll meet again, though, when I bring my mother to see the garden. She teaches Japanese,' he informed Kit, winking, as he made for the door.

As the sound of Simon's engine receded into the night, Kit and Daniel sat down again. Daniel read what was on the first of the new sheets, then handed it to Kit.

'What does it say?' asked Laura, who had drunk her coffee and returned to normal.

'It's another poem,' said Kit. 'Simon's written that it's a lullaby from Wakayama. It says,

> *You, orphan child,*
> *Bow to the setting sun,*
> *For there your parents are –*
> *In the sun, as she sets.*'

It seemed oddly familiar, until she realized that she was associating it with her first, never-to-be forgotten sight of the Japanese garden. The poem really meant nothing to her at all. But then, as she stared blankly at Daniel, she heard Laura say something which brought a most extraordinary solution to the mysteries into view.

'Hey, what a coincidence! Miss Sorley has a painting upstairs which could be an illustration of that poem. It's a bit like the one we had in the sitting-room at home, Kit, but it has people in it.'

'What people?' asked Kit, licking lips which had suddenly become dry.

'A Japanese man in a kimono,' replied Laura. 'Shadowy – a bit ghostly, even – among the pines. And beside the lake, looking towards the sunset, a little girl. At least, I suppose it's a coincidence,' she concluded uncertainly, catching sight of Kit and Daniel's astounded faces.

There was silence in the old kitchen where, on a spring morning long ago, the cook had rocked a foundling baby in her arms. Upstairs, Miss Sorley's clock struck eight.

As the last chime faded Daniel, who had been looking intently at Simon's final translation, raised his head and said soberly, 'It all hangs together, Puss.'

'Does it?'

'Yes. We know that Kojima was going to die, don't we, and that he was worried about leaving someone he loved? Well, this is his prayer to Inari, and it tells us who that someone was.'

He pushed the paper across the table to Kit, who

126

rather breathlessly read aloud, '"I think I shall die soon. Please look after my little daughter."'

'It must have been his little daughter he was thinking about when he carved the verse about the orphan child and the setting sun,' Daniel went on. 'The one about the pine at the peak of Inaba was his promise that he wouldn't leave her.'

The red sun and the pine. Motifs which appeared in Clare Sorley's paintings, time after time. But even with the truth staring her in the face, Kit couldn't accept it.

'It can't have been Miss Sorley,' she burst out. 'She was abandoned on the doorstep, for heaven's sake. Mrs Maxwell says no one knows who she is, not even Miss Sorley herself.'

But even as she spoke, Kit remembered the shawl with the word 'Yanagi' embroidered on it. 'Yanagi', Japanese for 'Green Willow', Miss Sorley's artist's name. And she noticed Laura shaking her head.

'No, you're wrong, Kit,' Laura said firmly. 'I dare say Mrs Maxwell doesn't know who Miss Sorley is, but Miss Sorley certainly does. The couple who made the Japanese garden were her grandparents.'

'Grandparents?' echoed Kit, bewildered by yet another unexpected turn of events. 'You mean, adopted grandparents?'

'No, real,' said Laura. 'When we were talking about her painting, she told me that the Sorleys produced one artist in every generation. She said that her great-grandmother, Lady Judith Vane, was a fine watercolourist, and that her grandmother, Hester Sorley, would have been another if she hadn't put all her energy into travelling, and creating the

Japanese garden. She also said –' Kit watched Laura's eyes move thoughtfully towards Daniel '– that she'd always wondered whether her mother was an artist too. But she never had the chance to find out. Her mother ran away to London just after Miss Sorley was born.' Laura paused, then she said with careful emphasis, 'One artist in every generation. Forgive me, Daniel – but are you absolutely sure your granny's maiden name was Maddimoss?'

# 20

# Judith
# Maddimoss

Under the pallid electric light, Kit saw that Daniel's face had gone very white. He stared at Laura with an expression of complete incredulity, which changed slowly to uncertainty, then suddenly to comprehension. He took a deep breath, and gulped audibly before he began to speak.

'It's what we all believed,' he said. 'That her name was Judith Maddimoss, and she'd come from Scotland to work in London when she was seventeen. Mum and Dad reckoned she'd left home to find a better job, although there was always a bit of a mystery about her. When I was little, Grandad used to tell me stories about the farm in Hampshire where he was brought up, but Granny never talked about her early life. I used to think she just wasn't interested in the past, but – well, recently I've wondered if she had another reason.'

Suddenly Kit remembered a remark Daniel had made on the day he arrived at Maddimoss. 'I'm looking for – I'm looking for a member of my granny's family.' There had been a tiny hesitation, and Kit had known he had gone back on what he had originally intended to say. Now she was certain that his quest was personal; he was not searching for just anyone called Maddimoss.

'Daniel, who exactly are you looking for?' she asked.

Daniel hesitated for a moment, but then he said, 'Right. I may as well come clean. After Grandad died in 1987, Granny came to stay with us. She was very old – eighty-eight when she died last year – and at the end of her life she was in bed most of the time, although she could still do her embroidery. Yes, she was an artist, all right. You can see her work in half a dozen churches round where we live.

'When I was at home in the holidays, I used to go and sit with her in the evenings. She liked that, and we had a lot of laughs. The last holiday before she died, though, I found her a bit confused. She kept calling me my dad's name, and telling me the same stories over and over, and talking about Grandad as if he was still alive. The night before I went back to school, she gave me a little parcel, and asked me to give it to her daughter. I told her she didn't have a daughter – my dad was an only son. Then she got all upset, and said she did have a daughter, in Scotland. I thought she said her name was "Aggie". Her speech wasn't very clear when she didn't have her teeth in.'

'Yanagi,' breathed Kit.

Daniel seemed to be shaking his head and nodding at the same time.

'I suppose it could have been,' he said. 'She kept saying, "Maddimoss, Gilbert. Look for Maddimoss." Gilbert's my dad's name. Anyway, when I promised that I would, she quietened down and fell asleep. I went back to school the next morning, and I never saw her again. At the time, I thought Granny was just losing her marbles through old age, but later, after she was dead, I began to wonder. I thought, if she'd had a baby before she was married, that would explain why she wouldn't talk about the past. People weren't very nice to single mothers in those days, were they?'

'No,' agreed Laura sombrely. 'And often their own parents were among the harshest and least forgiving. If Miss Sorley of Maddimoss was pregnant by the Japanese gardener, she probably had good reason for running away.'

'But why did she leave her baby?' cried Kit passionately. 'It was cruel. Why didn't she take it with her?'

She saw Daniel looking stricken, and wished she'd held her tongue.

But Laura said briskly, 'For two good reasons. Firstly, she had to look for work, and in those days no one would have employed an unmarried girl with a small child. Secondly, her parents were very rich. She knew they could give the baby security which she might never be able to provide. She didn't throw her baby away, Kit. It must have hurt her dreadfully to do what she did.'

As it must have hurt my mother to part with me, thought Kit guiltily. She hadn't forgotten her natural mother, and often had to stifle the feeling that, by deciding to stay with Laura, she had betrayed her. She stifled it again now.

'Have you still got the parcel?' she asked Daniel.

'It's in my rucksack,' he replied. 'When I knew I was coming to Scotland, I remembered what I'd promised Granny. I decided to bring the parcel, and see if I could find her daughter. But I've drawn a blank, which isn't surprising if Granny's name wasn't Maddimoss at all. She must have changed it because she wanted a new name for a new life.'

'But also wanted to keep a link with her past,' said Laura. 'So Judith Sorley became Judith Maddimoss.'

Something was coming back to Kit.

'Of course!' she exclaimed. 'I knew I'd heard that name before. Daniel, don't you remember? On one of the little gravestones at Frankly it said, "Jenny Cameron, nurse to Judith and Clare Sorley."'

Daniel looked dazed, as if he were still struggling to believe the impossible. He kept closing his eyes and shaking his head.

'It's the last thing I'd ever have thought of,' he said. 'Miss Sorley's an old woman. Could she really be my granny's daughter?'

This had seemed odd to Kit too, but Laura said, 'She's seventy-two. If your granny died aged eighty-eight, the child she had when she was seventeen would then have been seventy-one. As you say yourself, it hangs together.'

'I'll fetch the parcel,' Daniel said, and left the kitchen abruptly.

Kit looked across the table at Laura.

'Do you suppose people were nasty to my – that is, my original mother?' she asked awkwardly.

Laura shook her head.

'No. People are more enlightened now than they were seventy years ago,' she said gently. 'Whatever may be wrong with the modern world, in many ways it's a kindlier place.'

Daniel came back with a small brown-paper parcel, tied with blue thread. He put it down on the table.

'Should I open it?' he asked Laura, who said, 'That's up to you.'

'Well, I shall,' decided Daniel. 'If there's a message in it, maybe it will take away the queer feeling I have that this isn't really happening. If not, no harm's done. I can tie it up again afterwards.'

Kit thought she would choke with impatience as he fiddled with the knot, pulled off the thread and folded back the wrapping paper. In the parcel were a lacquered fan with a green silk tassel, and a small white card. Peering inquisitively over Daniel's shoulder, Kit read the tremulously written words, 'For my daughter Yanagi. Your father gave me this fan. With Mother's love.'

Kit smiled in satisfaction, but an almost comically thunderstruck expression appeared on Daniel's face.

'Jeeze!' he groaned. 'You know what this means, don't you? That old dame upstairs is my aunt. I'm a posh boy after all.'

# 21

# Kojima's
# Daughter

That night, for the first time in ages, Kit dreamed vividly. But her dream wasn't about Juliet, and afterwards she lay thinking not about the past, but the future.

The dream began in the Japanese garden at Maddimoss, on a breezy, bright spring day. Kit walked under the torii, but instead of following the familiar stepping-stones to Koraku-en, she found herself walking through an arcade of red lacquered torii, with silver slits of sky in between.

At the end of the arcade stood a shrine, larger and more ornate than the one at Maddimoss; as she stood in its forecourt, smiling at the red-bibbed foxes guarding its entrance, Kit realized that she was in Japan. In her hand she was holding a blank ema. Taking a pen from her pocket, she wrote on it, 'I want to live in Japan one day. Please help me to learn Japanese.' Then she hung up her ema in a little shelter beside Inari's shrine.

That was the dream that liberated Kit. When she woke she knew that from now on she would be able to love Daniel without needing to be with him every day. What she had said to Simon Heale hadn't been an idle boast, intended only to get herself attention.

She really did want to learn Japanese, and work as a teacher in Japan when she grew up. In her spare time she would visit shrines and gardens, and climb Mount Fuji, the sacred mountain of Japan. And perhaps, like Judith Sorley, she would fall in love with a handsome young Japanese.

In the morning, she found Daniel eating cornflakes in the kitchen with a strange, alert expression on his face.

'She's gone out with the dog,' he greeted Kit. 'When she comes back, off we go.'

He did his best to sound cool, but Kit sensed his excitement, and shared it. They would have gone upstairs to see Miss Sorley late last night, if Laura hadn't stopped them.

'If she's waited seventy-two years to learn the truth, she can wait a few hours more. So can you.'

Kit was finishing her toast and marmalade when she heard Miss Sorley calling, 'Beppo! Here, boy,' in the hall, then the sound of her door clicking shut at the top of the stair. Daniel drained his coffee mug and rose from the table.

'I've clipped the translations to the scrolls,' he told Kit. 'You take them, and I'll take the foxes.'

With her heart thumping, Kit followed him. Encouraged by Laura's successful visit, she was sure the old lady would be pleased to see them. Neither she nor Daniel was prepared for what happened next.

A wooden partition had been erected across the top of the stair, to separate Miss Sorley's flat from the rest of the house. When Daniel rang the bell, Beppo the spaniel began to bark hysterically. Through the frosted glass panel in the door, he and

Kit could see Miss Sorley struggling to catch hold of his collar and thrust him into a room. His noise was muffled as she shut him in, and the next moment she was facing them, hardly larger than a child in her brown tweed skirt and black jersey. Her eyes were invisible behind her dark glasses, but there was a frown between her brows, and her mouth was set in a line that was anything but welcoming. Over her shoulder Kit could see, against the pale chrysan-themum wallpaper from which she had made her scrolls, the painting of the Japanese gardener and his little girl. But Miss Sorley's attention was on Daniel, and his on her.

Kit heard Daniel say, 'We brought you these – um, presents,' and when he held out the foxes to Miss Sorley, she held out the scrolls. Miss Sorley didn't answer, but she took the gifts, and stood clasping them awkwardly against her chest. Kit thought she was going to say something, but the sound she made was inarticulate. She seemed frightened, and close to tears. With her arms full she backed away from them, caught the door with her foot and slammed it shut. Kit and Daniel were left crestfallen on the landing.

'She is loopy,' said Daniel gloomily as they went downstairs. But Laura, who was drinking coffee in her dressing gown, took a more relaxed view.

'You startled her,' she said. 'When she's had time to think she'll contact you, you'll see. Now why don't you go and work in your garden? It's going to be a lovely day.'

It was, and they did, working off their disappoint-ment by clearing an old path through iris and fern, and finding a flattened bamboo gate at the end of it.

'I must come back in the summer,' said Daniel, as they sat in the sunshine at the door of the derelict tea house, passing a bottle of orange juice between them. 'There's so much still to do.'

Kit recognized the note of desperation in his voice. He had finished working at Whitewells the previous day, and had been to Dundee to buy a train ticket. He had told his mother to expect him home on Wednesday, and time was running out. Oh, glory, thought Kit. Suppose Miss Sorley doesn't contact us?

That fear, however, was quickly blown away. When they arrived home for lunch, a note awaited them.

'Dear Kit and Daniel,
  Please forgive me for being so rude. I shall be delighted if you will come to tea with me this afternoon – about four o'clock, if that suits you.
                                        Yours sincerely,
                                        Clare Sorley.'

'It suits us, OK,' crowed Daniel jubilantly.

At three o'clock Kit had a shower, and put on the navy blue corduroy dress which Laura had bought her in Dundee. Daniel changed into clean jeans and a grey striped shirt. The clock was striking four as they climbed the stair for the second time that day. This time, when they rang the bell, Beppo's barking was distant, and they guessed that he had been banished to a room at the back of the house. Again they glimpsed Miss Sorley through the frosted glass, but not clearly enough to anticipate what they would see when she opened the door. When she did, they managed not to gasp audibly, but only just.

They had dressed specially for her, and she had dressed specially for them. Kojima's daughter was wearing a grey silk kimono, with a broad violet sash tied at her back in a large padded knot. Her narrow, shapely feet were in black sandals, and she had removed her spectacles, revealing dark eyes which were beautiful, and unmistakably Japanese. When she said, 'Good afternoon. Please come in,' her English voice seemed oddly at variance with her exotic appearance. But Kit and Daniel knew why she had dressed like this. She was saying, 'Look at me. This is who I am.'

As Kit remarked to Laura later, it was no wonder the downstairs flat of Maddimoss House was so over-crowded. The upstairs flat was almost empty. The sitting-room into which Miss Sorley led them was wide and airy, cream-carpeted and white-walled, with two tall, uncurtained windows. On a pale marble chimneypiece stood three white porcelain bowls; opposite hung a large green and grey painting of woodland, fields and a river. Kit felt herself blushing with pleasure when she saw two of her scrolls suspended in alcoves on either side of the fireplace. Below each was a white vase with a simple arrangement of larch and lemon narcissi. Kit no longer had to wonder who had put flowers on Kojima's grave.

There was a brown leather sofa and two small chests of drawers, but the only other furniture was a long, low table where the shrine foxes now sat, and three cream silk cushions, two on one side of the table and one on the other. Miss Sorley invited Kit and Daniel to sit down, saying, 'I suggest you sit cross-legged. Kneeling gets painful if you're not used to it.' She had removed her sandals at the door, and now knelt on the single cushion, sitting back on her feet. She watched in mild amusement as her guests sat down, trying not to fall off the cushions as they arranged their legs. But when they were settled she said seriously, 'I'm so sorry about this morning. I'm really very, very grateful.' Then, before they had time to answer, she went on, 'It would help me to understand what's been happening if you told me your story first. Then I'll gladly tell you mine. And please, call me Clare, because I don't think we'll be strangers for long.'

Kit had thought she was too astonished to speak, but now she heard herself asking, 'Not Yanagi?'

'No. No one has ever actually called me that,' Clare Sorley replied.

Daniel and Kit were surprised how easy it was to tell her about the shawl, and the photograph, and how they had gone to Frankly to find out the gardener's name. She listened intently as Kit recounted how they had found the ema and the writings in the shrine of Inari, and Daniel described the appearances of Kojima in Koraku-en. She showed no surprise, but smiled slightly and said, 'Oh, yes. I wondered when he was going to come into the story. Who translated the inscriptions?'

Kit explained how Simon had answered their advertisement, then she said shyly, 'Clare, when you read the poems and the ema, did they mean anything special to you?'

'Oh, yes. They meant everything to me,' said Clare fervently. She picked up one of the foxes, and drew her forefinger down his smooth back, and up his gilded tail. Then she went on, 'If you've lived for more than twenty minutes at Maddimoss, you must have heard how I first came to light howling my head off outside the back door. Whether the people here know who I really am, I've no idea.'

'They don't,' Kit assured her. 'Mrs Maxwell would have told me.'

Clare laughed right out at this.

'That I can well believe,' she said. 'However – the shawl you found in the box with the Sorley christening robe belonged to my mother. She had wrapped me in it and sewn on to it the Japanese name which she – and perhaps my father – had chosen for me. Yanagi, or Green Willow, was the heroine of a Japanese folk-tale called *The Irises of the Sixth Day*. She was famous for her great beauty.'

She smiled in mockery of her own lined face and grey hair, but when Daniel and Kit didn't smile too she went on with her story. 'My grandparents took me in and brought me up, and I must be grateful to them for that. But it was considered wrong and shameful in those days for an unmarried couple to have a child. My grandparents didn't love me, and they were terrified that if people saw me they would guess the truth. So they hid me away, and I spent my childhood in a kind of prison. I was looked after by Jenny Cameron, who had been my mother's nurse. Her daughter Ismay was the only other child I was ever allowed to play with.'

'Mrs Brown?' asked Kit.

'Yes. She's the only close friend I've ever had,' Clare replied. 'Every morning, Jenny used to take me for a walk in the grounds. We usually came back through the Japanese garden, where I saw a young Japanese gardener at work. I liked the kind way he smiled at me, but my grandmother had forbidden me to speak to him, and I know she had forbidden him to speak to me. The only time I ever disobeyed her and said, "Good morning, gardener," he bowed to me and said, "Kon ni chi wa, Ojoosan." Good morning, young mistress. I can scarcely bear to think about it. He was my father.'

Kit glanced away from the pain in Clare's eyes, but Daniel said, 'I'd have expected your grandparents to sack him. I thought posh people were good at that sort of thing,' he added bluntly.

Clare ignored the criticism, and answered the question.

'My grandparents were proud and hard, Daniel, but they felt responsible for the people who worked for them. They knew that if they dismissed my father, he would be alone and destitute in a strange land. Besides —' she sighed sadly '—I'm afraid they blamed my mother much more. They were furious with Judith because they were convinced that she had taken unfair advantage of my father's loneliness, and persuaded him to behave in a way his Japanese upbringing would have taught him to abhor. They were ashamed of her, and — perhaps because they loved Japan so much — unexpectedly sympathetic to him. They told everyone that Judith had died in a railway accident in France, and they never forgave her.'

Daniel said nothing, and Clare continued. 'As I grew up, I knew I was different from other people, but I didn't know why. I loved the things my grandparents had brought back from Japan, but I hated the cluttered, messy way they were displayed. I loved to arrange flowers, and I was thrilled by the books of Japanese prints in my grandfather's library. I suppose looking in a mirror should have told me the truth, but I'd no reason to think of it. It wasn't until I went to boarding school in England when I was nine, and one of the other girls said, "You're Japanese," that my suspicions were aroused. Then when I came home for the Christmas holidays, I heard that the Japanese gardener had died of tuberculosis just after I'd gone away. I tackled my grandmother, and she told me the whole story. She said it was my right to know. That was when I learned that my mother had run away from home when she discovered she was pregnant, and had only crept back to leave me on the doorstep. Later she wrote to tell her parents that she was in London.'

'But they never even tried to find her,' said Daniel harshly.

'No. I've never known what happened to her,' replied Clare. 'But –' she spoke with slight emphasis, looking straight at Daniel across the table '– I think probably you can tell me. You're the image of my grandfather. When I met you that day on the doorstep, you scared me half to death.'

Kit watched Clare sympathetically as Daniel told again the tale of Judith Maddimoss, who had toiled as a kitchen maid in Lord Pinkerton's London house, and married a footman called Thomas Garth. The lined, rather tired face showed little emotion, but when Daniel had finished, a faint smile of satisfaction curved the full lips.

'So she fell in love with another servant, and married him,' said Judith's daughter. 'Well, good for her. Only –' the smile faded '– I suppose I've always hoped she'd been faithful to my father. Silly, really.'

Kit heard Daniel gulp, the way he did when he was excited. When he spoke, his voice was strangely high.

'But she was faithful,' he said proudly, 'for as long as Kojima lived. Grandad had been asking her to marry him for years, but she'd always refused. Then one day in 1930, when she was in Hyde Park, a ghost came and walked beside her. We all knew about it, Clare. You can ask my dad when you meet him. Granny said the ghost was an old friend. He'd come to tell her that he was dead, and now she was free to marry if she wanted to. It must have been Kojima. Granny didn't marry Grandad till 1932.'

Clare said, 'Oh, my dear boy,' but Daniel hurried on.

'She didn't forget you, either. That's why I'm here. Before she died last year, she asked me to come to Scotland and find her daughter. She sent you a present.' Daniel put his hand into the pocket of his jeans, and took out the little parcel. 'This is it,' he concluded breathlessly, and pushed it across the table.

Kit knew she was going to cry. She watched Clare's trembling fingers undoing the parcel, lifting out the fan and the little card. Then, when Daniel scrambled impulsively round the table to give Clare a hug, she took out her handkerchief, wiped her eyes and blew her nose. She felt her happiness was now complete.

# 22

# Daniel Garth's
# Inheritance

The clock in the hall struck five, and Clare said it
was high time they had tea.

'One day I'll teach you the Japanese tea
ceremony,' she promised, 'but ordinary tea will do
for today.'

She went to release Beppo from his temporary
prison, and Kit and Daniel made friends with him
while she made herself a pot of tea, and took Coke
and sandwiches out of the 'fridge for them. When
they were sitting, relaxed and friendly, round the
kitchen table, Clare took up her story again.

'After the Christmas when my grandmother told
me about my parents,' she said, 'I didn't visit Maddimoss again for many years. My grandfather bought
a house in London, and I spent my holidays there
until I left school. Then I studied art in Paris, and
later lived in London in a studio of my own. I
suppose I was successful, and I met a lot of people,
but I didn't make friends easily, and I wasn't happy.
I felt divided, as if I didn't know who I really was.
When I signed my work "Yanagi" I was saying, "I
am Japanese," but I'd never been to Japan, and
knew only a few words of the language. Then in
World War II, the British and Japanese fought

against each other. I knew where my loyalty lay, but sometimes I felt I was being torn in two.

'My grandfather died in 1940, but my grandmother lived until 1953. After her death I discovered that she'd left me everything – this house, farms, land and a great deal of money. People said enviously how fortunate I was, but I'd have given it all for one affectionate word when she was alive. However, being rich meant that I could travel. I put a manager in charge of Maddimoss, and in 1954 I went to Japan for a year.'

'Did you like it?' asked Kit eagerly, but Clare ruefully shook her head.

'I didn't find what I was looking for,' she said. 'In London, I'd felt Japanese. In Tokyo, I felt European. Oh, I loved the gardens of Okayama and Kyoto, and the shrines and the torii and the plum blossom. But I felt like a tourist where I wanted to be at home. The worst part was visiting Hiroshima, where an atomic bomb had been dropped eight years before.' There was hurt in her eyes again, and a faint colour touched her pale cheeks. 'Eighty thousand people were killed in an instant,' she added with scarcely concealed anger. 'Whatever the rights and wrongs of war, I can't believe that should ever have happened.'

'Too right,' agreed Daniel forcefully, but Kit said, 'Of course. Kojima came from Hiroshima. It was in the book you lent us.'

'Yes,' said Clare. 'I didn't expect to find any trace of him. I didn't even know his full name. But knowing that every single thing he'd ever looked at was wiped out forced me to accept that I had no roots in Japan either.'

'So you came back,' Daniel said.

'I did. I lived in London until five years ago, when the worst thing that can happen to an artist happened to me. I began to go blind.' There wasn't a scrap of self-pity in her voice, and Kit sensed that sympathetic noises would be unwelcome. She let Clare get on with her story.

'I had several operations, and after the last one the surgeon said my sight probably wouldn't get any worse. I could still see a certain amount, but I knew I'd never paint again. I felt tired and ill, and my doctor advised me to go somewhere quiet for a while. After a lot of hesitation, I decided to come to Maddimoss. On one hand, I hadn't lived here since I was ten, and I had no happy memories. On the other, the people who had rented this flat had left, and Ismay was here. We'd always kept in touch, and I knew she'd look after me. So I came, meaning to stay three months. But it wasn't easy to go away. The first time I took Beppo for a walk in that neglected old Japanese garden, I discovered that Ismay wasn't the only friend I had at Maddimoss.'

'Kojima,' breathed Kit. 'You saw him too.'

'Yes, indeed. He'd been waiting for me for close on sixty years.'

'Did he speak to you?' asked Daniel curiously.

'No, never. But for a long time I saw him almost every day. In the house, I'd be sorting out old photographs and there he was. Out of doors, I met him constantly. I knew he was trying to tell me something, but I'd no idea what it was.'

'Were you afraid?' inquired Daniel.

'No, of course not.' Clare sounded a little impatient. 'Why should we be afraid of ghosts?'

'That's what I say,' Daniel agreed.

'What I felt wasn't fear,' Clare explained. 'It was distress because I couldn't find out what my father wanted me to know. He used to stand – he so young, and I so old – at the torii, and beckon me into Koraku-en. But when I went in, all I could see was the bell from Miyajima and the old shrine full of leaves. Then he stopped appearing so often, and I thought he'd given up on me.' She smiled impishly. 'It seems he was waiting for less dim-witted people to turn up.'

'But why us?' asked Kit, who had never found a satisfactory answer to this question.

Clare at least took it seriously.

'All I can suggest,' she said, 'is that – because of what he is – he knows things we don't know. Perhaps he foresaw the coming of Judith Sorley's grandson. Perhaps he simply saw you and Daniel in the garden, and knew that you were friends he could trust. He would certainly sense that you were good, and re-sourceful and brave. Also, he has a mysterious power to put ideas into people's minds. I know that from my own experience.'

She poured herself another cup of tea, and looked intensely at Kit and Daniel. 'When I was young,' she told them, 'I was obsessed with two symbols, the pine tree and the dying sun. Without knowing why, I painted them over and over again. Only this morn-ing, when I read the poems you brought me, did I realize that the answer had been here at Maddimoss all the time. But how my father's thoughts, in the last days of his short life, were transferred into my paintings, I really can't begin to understand.'

'Did you pine for him?' asked Kit, remembering the words,

> *If I hear you pine for me*
> *I shall return to you.*

'Yes, I did,' Clare replied. 'Always.'

'Then I wonder why he didn't appear to you in London, like he did to Granny,' mused Daniel.

'Because,' said Clare with certainty, 'the proof that he loved me was in the shrine at Maddimoss. I had to come back here to find my parents, *in the sun, as she sets.*'

She sounded so happy that Kit felt she was going to cry again. So she blinked and said quickly, 'The clue was in the book you lent us. Your grandmother wrote that she'd bawled Kojima out for wasting time carving in the shrine. Did you never read it?'

Clare smiled, obviously relishing the words 'bawled out'. Then she shook her head.

'I've glanced through it, but I can't see well enough to read much,' she explained, adding, 'So that's what put you on the trail. I did wonder.'

'So why did you send such a cross note to Laura when we asked if you knew what the inscriptions meant?' demanded Kit, then wondered if she'd gone too far.

But really it was hard to recognize the notoriously cool, aloof Miss Sorley in Clare, perched on a cushion on a kitchen chair, chatting and warming her hands on her teacup. Clare looked slightly embarrassed, but she didn't apologize.

'I was afraid,' she said. 'Seeing Daniel had upset

me, and I was worried about what you might un-
cover. If you have a past like mine, you dread having
it dug up. I know the people here think I'm snooty
and peculiar, but I hate being the object of so much
curiosity.'

'If they knew the truth, they wouldn't have anything to be curious about,' Daniel pointed out, rather
daringly.

'There's logic in that,' said Clare noncommit-
tally.

Daniel and Kit helped her to wash up, then they
all drifted back to the sun-washed sitting-room.
Daniel and Kit sat on the floor, while Clare curled
up on the sofa with Beppo at her feet.

'You had better admire my finery today,' she
warned them. 'You won't see it again for a long
time. Japanese clothes are beautiful, but a great knot
in the middle of my back doesn't suit my lazy
habits.'

They sat in companionable silence for a while,
then Kit said, 'Clare, do you suppose we'll ever see
Kojima again?'

Clare was fondling Beppo's ears, and seemed to
consider before replying, 'No. I don't think so, Kit.
I'm sure he waited until he knew I had received his
message, but now – well, he's free. In an odd way,
so am I. I kept the Japanese garden untouched because of him, but –' She broke off suddenly, gasped,
and sat bolt upright. Then she shivered and to their
horror Daniel and Kit saw her go so white they
thought she was going to faint. 'Oh, God,' she
moaned. 'What have I done?'

Kit hurried over to her, and took her hand.

'It's all right, Clare,' she said soothingly, but Clare was staring at Daniel.

'No, it isn't,' she whispered. 'Oh, Daniel! I've just realized. I've sold your inheritance.'

Daniel stared back. It was plain that he hadn't a clue what she meant.

'Inheritance?' he repeated blankly. 'What inheritance? I don't understand.'

Clare made an effort, and controlled herself, but kept hold of Kit's hand.

'The estate of Maddimoss,' she explained miserably. 'It ought to have belonged to your grandmother, who would have passed it on to your father, and he to you. But I've sold everything, except Sparrowlea farmhouse and the Japanese garden.'

Fortunately, Daniel's reaction to this tragedy was to put back his head and burst out laughing.

'Jeeze, is that all?' he chortled. 'Then forget it. Dad's got loads of money, and he's never done preaching at me that I'll have to work for mine. If you'd rather have the cash than a lot of old ruins, good luck to you. No sweat.'

Clare let Kit's hand go, and leaned against the arm of the sofa. Her relief was palpable, but she was stung by Daniel's words, and hurried to explain.

'I didn't want the money for myself,' she assured him. 'Because I believed I had no heirs, I decided to turn this house into a centre where young British and Japanese artists could come for a year or two, to live and work together. Some people I knew in London agreed to become trustees, but as well as giving the house, I've had to provide most of the funds. It will cost a lot to convert this place into studios and living quarters, and some artists will need financial help. So I needed all the cash I could rake together.

'Now it's all arranged. Last week in London I signed the papers. In September I'm moving into Sparrowlea farmhouse with Ismay, and I hope the first artists will arrive here next spring. We've got a long waiting-list already.' As she spoke, Clare's face had become young and bright with enthusiasm, but now it darkened again. 'All the same, I wish I'd known about you sooner,' she said.

But Daniel's grin was splitting his face from ear to ear.

'That,' he said, 'is the most brilliant idea I've ever heard. Pure magic. Am I allowed to put my name on the waiting-list now?'

Clare leaned towards him.

'You're an artist?' she asked keenly.

'Well, not like you,' Daniel said. 'But I want to be. Dad would prefer me to be a doctor, but I decided last night. Laura told us you said the Sorleys produced one artist in every generation. If it's me in my generation, I can't do anything else. That's my inheritance, isn't it?'

# 23

## *Adopted*
## *Children*

After breakfast the following morning, Daniel went
up to Whitewells Farm to tell his story, and Clare's,
to Mr and Mrs Maxwell. After some indecision,
Clare had agreed that it would be better to tell the
truth than to risk even wilder rumours circulating.

'I suppose if Mrs Maxwell knows,' she said, 'the
story will get around faster than if I send it to the
*Dundee Courier.*'

Kit was taken aback by the tartness of this remark,
until she remembered all the waspish things Mrs
Maxwell had said about Clare. She hoped that, once
the truth was known, a truce might follow.

Meanwhile, with Daniel out of the way, Kit
thought she would go up and visit Clare on her own.
Last night she had come down at seven, but Daniel
had stayed on much later, telling Clare about his
family and discussing his future. Kit wasn't exactly
jealous; she knew that Daniel's desire to make a
good impression on his famous relation was the best
guarantee that he would stop doing silly things. Still,
she felt a little left out, and thought it would be nice
to talk to Clare without Daniel butting in all the
time. So at ten o'clock she went upstairs and rang
the bell. This time she heard Beppo's barking

silenced by a firm command, and tall, dark-haired Mrs Brown opened the door.

'Please, may I see Clare?' asked Kit, while Beppo ran out and rubbed his curly body warmly against her leg.

'Oh, it's "Clare", is it?' said Mrs Brown, giving Kit a look which was half disapproving and half amused. 'Well, I'm not sure. She isn't dressed yet.' But then, seeing Kit's disappointment, she relented. 'Still, she might like a visitor. I'll go and ask her.'

She disappeared into the sitting-room, and Kit knelt down to make a fuss of Beppo. Mrs Brown soon returned.

'You're to come in,' she said, holding the door open.

Clare was sitting on the sofa with her feet up, drinking coffee and listening to the radio. She switched it off, and curled up on her feet to make room for Kit. Kit thought how different she looked today, in her white nightie and plaid dressing gown, with her hair loosely plaited and tied with brown ribbon. Not mysterious, not famous, not even very Japanese. Just an ordinary old lady enjoying a leisurely Sunday morning.

'You must excuse me,' she said. 'I wasn't expecting company. But I'm glad you've come, because I want to talk to you about something.'

'You do?'

Kit, who wanted to talk to her about something, was surprised.

'Yes. We had so many things to discuss yesterday, I didn't thank you properly for all your work in the Japanese garden, or for the scrolls, or for trying to save the shrine when the vandals came. Daniel told me last night that you were hurt. I didn't know, and I'm very sorry.'

'Oh, I'm fine now,' Kit assured her. 'It was Kojima who was heroic. He saved Daniel and me from an awful beating-up.'

It was strange, she thought, how natural it had become to talk of Kojima, not as a terrifying apparition, but as one of themselves. Clare nodded thoughtfully.

'Kit,' she said, 'I'd like to give you and Daniel a present to thank you for all you've done for me. I wondered if you'd like to have the Japanese garden.'

'The Japanese garden?' echoed Kit, not quite understanding.

Clare explained.

'I've never been able to have any repair work done there, for fear of distressing – the spirit. But now I'm going to have the shrine rebuilt, then Laura's wonderful foxes can go home. And because I have your scrolls, even my father's carvings can be replaced. We'll restore the tea house and the summer house, and find a gardener to look after the place. But I want it to belong to you and Daniel. I'll ask my lawyer to draw up a paper, passing the ownership from me to you. Would you like that?'

Kit was speechless. She felt her mouth opening and shutting like a fish's, but at last she swallowed hard, and managed to say, 'Oh, wouldn't I? I'd love it. Only –' she almost choked on the words '– I may not be here for long.'

'Oh, Kit!' Clare was surprised and disappointed.

'Why not? I thought your father was going to work in Dundee.'

'Yes, he was,' replied Kit dully. 'But now he's in Australia, and Laura's had a letter saying he wants to stay, and marry someone he's met in Sydney.'

'Oh, Lord,' said Clare, horrified. 'Poor Laura! Is she very upset?'

'A bit, I suppose,' Kit told her. 'But she saw it coming, and she says we all need a new start. She's going to look for a job. The biggest problem's the house Peter was having built. Mr Cameron, the builder, just won't get on with it, and Laura says if we have to be out of here by September, maybe we'll have to move – far away.' Kit's eyes filled with tears. It was all very well planning to go to Japan far in the future, but now she wanted to be with her new friends. 'I don't want to go,' she whispered.

Clare reached out and patted her hand.

'You don't have to,' she said firmly. 'I wouldn't leave you and Laura without a roof over your heads. And as for that Ned Cameron –' her voice was indignant '– you can leave him to me. He's Ismay's nephew, and even she says he's a rascal. I'll 'phone him tomorrow and tell him that if your house isn't ready in six weeks, he won't bang in a single nail when we come to convert this place. That'll put the wind up him, you'll see.' She smiled at Kit and said, 'I do want you to stay. Daniel is talking about living with me at Sparrowlea and going to art school in Dundee on the bus. I've told him he must talk it over with his parents, but he seems very determined. I just assumed you would be here too. However, to own the Japanese garden, you don't have to stay at

Maddimoss for ever. It only means you won't come back one day and find it's disappeared.'

Mrs Brown brought the coffee pot, and a cup for Kit. When she'd gone, Kit found words to thank Clare. Then she said, 'Please, may I ask you something?'

'Oh, dear,' said Clare teasingly. 'Don't tell me you want to be an artist too.'

'No way,' replied Kit. 'I'm going to work in Japan. Laura says I can have Japanese lessons, and I'm going to practise on your artists.'

Her spirits rose with the thought that this now seemed much more probable than it had fifteen minutes ago.

'Good idea. So, what do you want to ask me about?' asked Clare.

Kit was silent for a moment, but Clare's smile encouraged her, and she began to tell; how she had been adopted and given to Juliet as a Christmas present, how she had hated Juliet and felt unloved, how guilty she had felt when Juliet died. Then she told Clare what she couldn't tell anyone else, how she had longed for her natural mother, and been determined that she would find her one day.

'I know I was wrong about a lot of things,' she concluded. 'Laura does love me, and I love her, and I'm going to stick by her. But I can't forget my real mother, and I can't help wondering if she regrets letting me go. Perhaps I should still try to find her. What do you think?'

Clare leaned back in the corner of the sofa, and studied Kit with an odd expression in her myopic brown eyes. For an awful moment Kit thought she was going to duck out of answering, but then she said, 'I think the most important thing is to be clear about what may happen if you do. Of course you have the right to know who your parents were. Everyone has that right. But if you are imagining some close mother and daughter relationship, then frankly, I think you're inviting heartache. Your natural mother must now be nearly thirty. Probably she's married to someone who isn't your father, and who may not know you exist. Probably she has other children. You aren't part of her life, and there's no reason to suppose she'd welcome you with open arms.'

Although they were gently spoken, these seemed hard words to Kit.

'Your mother didn't forget you,' she pointed out, with a hint of reproach. 'She sent you a present after more than seventy years.'

Clare smiled wryly.

'I know,' she said, 'and you mustn't think I'm not glad, and grateful. But a happy ending doesn't rub out a sad story, Kit. I've never blamed my mother for what she did. She was in a pitiable position. But the fact is that she went to London, and made a new life for herself in which she didn't want to be reminded of me. She had seventy years to find me, but she never tried. She kept her past a secret from her husband, and her son. Only when she was an old, old woman, at the age when the distant past becomes much more vivid than the present, did she begin to grieve over the baby she'd left on a doorstep so long ago. Find out who your parents were if you must, my dear. But my advice is to settle for what you have.'

Sadness for Clare, and relief for herself, swept over

Kit. She knew that this was the counsel she had really wanted to hear.

'I'll leave it till I'm grown up,' she said gruffly, 'and see how I feel then. Thanks for helping me.' Then, noticing how tired Clare suddenly looked, she got up and said, 'I'd better push off now. But am I allowed to come and see you again?'

'Any more silly questions?' inquired Clare. Kit grinned and said goodbye. She was nearly at the door when she was called back. 'Kit, wait a minute.'

'Yes?'

Kit turned, and saw Clare looking alert again.

'You said that Laura was going to look for a job. What kind of job?'

Kit came back to the sofa.

'Anything, I suppose,' she said. 'She used to be a teacher, yonks ago. Why?'

'I wondered if perhaps she'd like to work for me.'

'For you?' Kit whistled. 'Doing what?'

Clare looked slightly abashed.

'I know it's ridiculous,' she said, 'but when I started this art centre business I had no idea what I was taking on. There's a colossal amount of paper-work, which I can't see properly, and soon I'll have to start going to Edinburgh, where the trustees are to meet. Ismay's convinced I'll be killed in the street if I don't have someone to steer me across, and after London last week, I agree with her. Then there'll be so much to do when the centre actually opens. I was going to advertise for someone to help me, but if you think Laura might – would you go and ask her, Kit?'

'I'm going,' shrieked Kit, already at the door.

That evening, in the luminous hour before dark, Daniel and Kit went for a walk in the Japanese garden, which was soon to be theirs. It was cold but tranquil, with tiny yellow irises fluorescent among the stones, and a chalk-white lace of blossom against the dark grey wood. The two friends were in contented mood.

'I'm glad your dad took your news so well,' remarked Kit, as they ambled along beside the faintly rippling lake.

Daniel had spent a long time that afternoon talking to his parents on the telephone.

'Mn. Apparently he'd been expecting it,' replied Daniel. 'He said it was my life, and he wished me well. Mind you,' he suddenly spluttered, 'I reckon he'd have howled louder if he hadn't been even more gobsmacked than Mrs Maxwell about Clare. Hopping up and down he was, at the way his dear old ma had deceived him.'

Kit giggled, but, 'He will be nice to Clare?' she asked anxiously.

'Fear not, Puss. At first he was tying himself in a knot at the thought of how posh she'd be, but I said she wasn't, and when I pointed out that her dad was a servant too, he cooled. He and Mum are coming to stay over Easter, and on Saturday they're throwing a party for us all.'

It had been a good day all round. After lunch Laura had gone up to see Clare, and had returned looking happy but bemused.

'If anyone had told me twenty years ago,' she said to Kit, 'that one day I'd be Clare Sorley's personal assistant, I'd have thought they were crazy.' Then she shook her head slowly, and added, 'Strange, though, isn't it? I'd always imagined she'd be as brilliant and exuberant as her paintings, not a shy little woman who needs a friend to hold her hand.'

The moon began to seep light through the conifer branches, and at the head of the lake Beppo ran out from the rhododendrons. He was followed by Clare, in her grey overcoat and a red scarf. While Beppo scampered off in pursuit of imaginary rabbits, she walked between Kit and Daniel past the waterfalls and the bridge where Kojima had been photographed two years after he died. Casually, she showed them things.

'That stone basin is where you cleanse your hands and mouth before the tea ceremony. When the tea house is restored, we'll put it to use. And look, this stone is a moon-viewing seat. We'll celebrate the moon festival on the fifteenth of August. That flat stone is called the Stone of Amusement. My grandfather used to fish from it until one day he slipped and fell in the water. He wasn't amused at all . . .'

Night was falling fast. A wild duck took off from the reeds, and headed up the lake in a shudder of invisible wings. Clare paused under the torii at the entrance to Koraku-en. She had been laughing, but suddenly her voice sounded forlorn.

'I was right, wasn't I? Even when I couldn't see him, I always felt him near. But he's gone, and the garden's empty. I didn't think I'd mind so much.'

'You have us now,' Daniel said.